THANKS ERNIE

JUMPMAN

RULE #1: DON'T TOUCH ANYTHING

GLAD YOU LIKED IT!

JAMES VALENTINE

ALADDIN PAPERBACKS
New York London Toronto Sydney

FOR JOANNE

ALADDIN PAPERBACKS
An imprint of Simon & Schuster Children's Publishing Division
1230 Avenue of the Americas, New York, NY 10020

Also available in a Simon and Schuster Books for Young Readers hardcover edition.
The text of this book was set in MetaPlus Roman.
Manufactured in the United States of America
First published in 2002 by Random House Australia Pty Ltd
Published by arrangement with Random House Australia Pty Ltd
First U.S. edition, 2004
First Aladdin Paperbacks edition June 2005
10 9 8 7 6 5 4 3 2 1
The Library of Congress has cataloged the hardcover edition as follows:
Valentine, James, 1961–
Jumpman rule #1 : don't touch anything / James Valentine.—1st U.S. ed.
p. cm.
Summary: When a defective time-jumping device strands Theodore, a teen from the distant future, in the twenty-first century, he is helped by two high schoolers—Jules, who is having time problems of his own, and Gen, an old friend Jules was about to ask out.
ISBN 0-689-86872-3 (hc.)
[1. Time and space—Fiction. 2. Science fiction.] I. Title: Jumpman rule number one. II. Title.
PZ7.V252Jt 2005 [Fic]—dc22 2004017603
ISBN 0-689-86877-4 (Aladdin pbk.)

Meanwhile . . .

"**WE LISTENED.** We heard what you were saying. And we came up with an answer. That answer is the Time-Master JumpMan Pro."

Quincy Carter One nodded to the crowd which was showing its appreciation in the usual way. It was puffing in and out very rapidly, making a *wuhwuhwuh* type of noise. Quincy adopted an expression that was both confident and remorseful.

"I'm sorry. We're all sorry. You were right. The JumpMan 70 was flashy and fiddly. It lost the classic simplicity of the JumpMan 60 and replaced it with a lot of features that you couldn't use and you didn't need. Frankly, it slurped!"

The crowd puffed even harder. *Wuhwuhwuhwuhwuh*! It sounded like a room full of asthmatic seals. But they were loving this. Here was the boss of the biggest company anywhere saying what they'd all been saying for years.

"As one of the original TimeMaster Six, as Cheeo of the

TimeMaster Corporation, I should have known better. But we can all learn from our mistakes and I'm sure—no, I know—that the TimeMaster JumpMan Pro is the kind of JumpMan for today's people and meets today's Time-Jumping needs."

The crowd lifted the volume. At the podium, Quincy Carter One felt their enthusiastic exhaling on his round red cheeks. They loved Quincy and they were all wuhing like crazy people.

"So let's launch the JumpMan Pro and let's jump!"

On stage, this week's music sensation SoundVat kicked into their hit, and everyone went crazy. Giant screens unfurled from the ceiling, filled with exhilarating and astonishing images and people caught their *wuhs* in amazement and went quiet.

Everyone on the two planets and probably even on the Moon is watching this, thought Quincy, a rich glow of satisfaction and anticipation flooding through him as he rocked back and forth on the balls of his feet, the creator and center of it all.

Was there a kid anywhere who hadn't entered this competition? First Jump with the new model to a brand-new JumpSite? Great prize, and they'd all wanted it.

Behind Quincy a giant clear sphere in the shape of JumpMan descended. Inside it names were appearing, as

TimeMaster computers flashed through the database of competition entrants. Precisely at midnight it would stop scrolling randomly through the millions of names and the name it stopped on would be the winner.

The crowd started counting down.

"Ten, nine, eight, seven . . ."

They counted it off exactly together. If there was one thing these people knew about, it was time.

"Three, two, one . . ."

Midnight.

The place went absolutely silent.

No music. No fanfare. No drumroll. Just a single spotlight on the short fat figure of Quincy Carter One, and a single name in the center of the sphere shining through the darkness.

"Theodore Pine Four!" read out Quincy, and the place exploded.

"Get that boy in a pod and get him down here!" Quincy's chubby, happy face was beaming.

Ten minutes later, after the crowd had enjoyed SoundVat playing their hit a few more times Theodore Pine Four arrived at the headquarters of TimeMaster and walked on stage to shake the hand of Quincy Carter One, the creator of the thing he loved most in the world, the JumpMan.

meanwhile > > >

Quincy beamed at Theo and then turned to the Vice Cheeo in charge of Publicity, Honeydew Meloni.

Honeydew leaned forward. "Yes?" she said. She was in charge of this launch. It was the biggest event anyone had ever seen and she'd organized it down to the color of the napkins in the VIP lounge, and there was nothing on her notes about the boss turning to her with a desperate look on his face.

"Where is it?" Quincy hissed.

"What?"

"The JumpMan! Where is it?"

"You were bringing it!" Honeydew felt faint, knowing that it was now her fault that the JumpMan wasn't there.

"It's in my office! Get it!"

As Honeydew ran off the stage and into the building, it occurred to her that the normally cheery, happy, extremely affable Quincy had just looked at her like he'd like to torture her very slowly. It was a look that was very un-Quincy.

The offices were deserted. Everyone was at the launch.

She thought the JumpMan would be obvious, but there was no sign of it. She searched the reception area, desperation levels rising. She would never normally have done this, but she couldn't go back empty-handed, so she went through into Quincy's office. Nothing obvious there either. She pulled open drawers and cupboards and without thinking about it she searched through the drawers in Quincy's desk.

There! In the bottom drawer, tucked behind some files, a JumpMan and a remote. That must be it. She wondered vaguely why the boss had thought he needed to hide it, but she didn't care. She just knew she'd left them all standing on the stage now for some minutes and the only hope she might have of saving her job was to get back there with a JumpMan as quickly as possible.

When she ran back onto the stage there was no sign of the Quincy Carter One who had wished her extreme pain earlier. It was the familiar old Quincy. Chirpy, funny, and full of old tales about the early days, and the crowd lapping them up, even though they'd heard it all before. They were great stories, and hearing them from one of the original TimeMaster Six, the only one really still around, was quite a treat.

"All right!" declared Quincy, raising his hands and bringing everyone back to the reason they were all there. "Sorry for the slight technical hitch. Having a launch of the greatest model JumpMan yet without the actual JumpMan was a fun idea for a while, but here it is, finally, the TimeMaster JumpMan Pro and Theodore Pine, it's all yours!"

Music started up, a specially commissioned brand-new symphony, and SoundVat slunk off, looking a bit peeved at being upstaged. The crowd went wild with delight, and Theodore Pine took the new JumpMan from Quincy.

It looked pretty much the same as his old one.

He picked up the bright red remote control and looked at it. The layout was a little different, but again, it was similar to his old JumpMan 70. Theodore realized that Quincy was talking to him.

"Just point the remote at the thing, and it'll take you to the most exciting JumpSite you've ever seen. You'll be the first one to see it, and we can't wait to hear what you think. Come back in five minutes?"

Theodore pointed the remote at the JumpMan. He closed his eyes, found the Go button, and pressed it.

chapter one

Bad Timing

Time. Time's a funny thing, thought Jules.

How come a minute can seem like forever or no time at all? How come when you're having a good time, time flies? Flies where? he wondered.

~ *Focus, his brain suggested. Remember what you came here to do.*

I don't want to remember, thought Jules.

~ *Stop reminding me, he told his brain.*

It's a rule, isn't it, thought Jules watching his foot take forever to climb one more stair. Start having fun and time speeds up. I wonder if you could reach a point where you're having so much fun that whatever you're doing appears to take no time at all?

Because the reverse is certainly true, he thought, pausing before dragging his other foot up one more stair. Start having a lousy time, and time doesn't fly anymore. It comes into land and then gets bogged in a swamp at the end of the runway.

His first day at Rosemount High, for example. There was a day that lasted a decade. How can time speed up and slow down like that? Or is it me that's doing the speeding up and slowing down?

~ *Could you stop this please? asked his brain. This kind of thinking causes me a lot of pain.*

~ *Sorry, said Jules.*

~ *It's OK. I'm your brain. You're just trying to make me think about time so you don't have to think about why you're climbing these stairs.*

That's the trouble with brains, Jules thought. They know exactly what you're not thinking.

~ *Good trick, isn't it?*

Jules Santorini, aged thirteen and a bit, was a thoughtful boy. Not thoughtful as in mowing the lawn for grandmothers kind of thoughtful, although he did do a bit of that, but thoughtful in that he was full of thoughts. Last week he'd been preoccupied with size. He'd been watching ants. I'm a giant to them, he thought, and they don't even really know I'm here. Maybe to something I can't even see, I'm just like an ant. He'd lost himself with that little contemplation for a week.

He never really stopped thinking, and he often found himself chatting with his brain. Or at least he thought it was his brain. Perhaps it was really his left earlobe just pretending to be his brain.

~ *Oh, please. Don't confuse me with those irrelevant fleshy lumps hanging off the side of your head! I am the most extraordinary thing on the entire planet. I am your brain, said his brain. But you're just doing it again. Avoiding what's happening. Thinking about the impossible. Why don't you think about what you're going to say, when you get to the top of these stairs?*

Jules knew his brain was right. He was trying to avoid the next few minutes. Wouldn't it be great if you could just fast forward through any of life's awkward bits and then pause on the good bits? Could you make time work like that? he wondered.

Jules Santorini, about five feet six inches tall, was a boy who felt perfectly ordinary. He didn't think he was good-looking, but he knew he wasn't ugly. His eyes seemed to be the normal distance apart. His nose appeared to be the standard model, not pointy, or snubby or flat across half his face. His teeth were mainly straight but he might get braces next year. His chin had a faint cleft in it, but not enough that anyone would ever really notice. He wasn't the tallest, the shortest, the fattest, the thinnest, the fastest, the slowest, the smartest, the dumbest.

In fact the only area where Jules was special was in his thoughts. He was far more thoughtful than most. Not that he realized this, of course. He thought everyone thought what he thought. Which is what everyone thinks. Unless they think nobody thinks what they think. Which is what everyone else thinks.

~ *Chicken, said his brain, sounding just like Max, who'd put him up to this in the first place.*

~ *I'm not chicken, lied Jules, who'd never felt more terrified in his entire life.*

~ *We're here, announced his brain.*

Jules had finally dragged his feet to the top of the stairs. Ahead of him was a door. Behind the door was Genevieve Corrigan. He'd known her forever. Or if not quite forever, at least since they were about three when he'd shared a bath with her and her sixteen Barbies. He didn't really remember that, he'd just seen the photo in his mother's album, the one she now kept in a box at the back of her cupboard.

Jules had been away living with his mother for the last two years and when he came back, he thought he and Gen would be friends again. But instead she was treating him like everyone else. He was the new kid. And new kids were not to be spoken to. Not by girls who'd attained cool status and who were part of what everyone recognized as the top gang. Jules thought Gen, Sonja, Kyeela, and Bonnie, who were now inseparable, were less of a gang and more of a whispering, sniggering, four-headed monster.

Why had he come back? Why was he doing this?

His hand was reaching out to knock on the door.

I can't, he thought, pulling his hand back. She'll just say no. She'll tell everyone.

~ *Chicken, his brain said. Chickenchickenchicken . . .*

~ *Thanks for your support, brain, said Jules to his brain. As soon as they invent brain transplants, I'm becoming a donor.*

~ *Oooooh, I'm scared! said his brain.*

From downstairs Jules could hear his dad, Tony, laughing with Gen's parents, Steven and Katherine. He could have stayed down there, pretending politely to be interested in their reminiscing. But no, instead he embarked on this fateful climb to Gen's bedroom, perhaps his only chance to see her alone, and to show Max that he could ask a girl out if he wanted to. And he did want to. Or did he?

He took a deep breath, raised his fist to knock again, and the door opened.

Genevieve Corrigan, aged nearly fourteen, a little bit taller than Jules, had dark straight hair that was exactly what any girl who wanted dark straight hair would want. Gen wanted long blonde hair that cascaded in waterfall-like waves and she felt unreasonably envious whenever she saw any girl who had that. She wished she didn't have that desire, and suspected it came from playing Sleeping Beauty with Jules for way too long when they were little. She also wished she was someone who didn't care about her hair. She hated the way she loved the way her hair shushed perfectly from side to side when she walked. Particularly if she used expensive, luxurious shampoo. Which she knew was tested on dogs and probably the few remaining pandas in the world and that she shouldn't ever want to use it again, but nothing else made her hair shush from side to side like the good stuff.

So what should she do? No one else seemed worried about these kind of things. They just worried about their hair. Gen felt sometimes like she was the only one who tried to grapple with these issues and so she was often more than a little angry. It wasn't fair and Gen had a lot of issues with fairness. She wanted everything to be fair—including her hair—but she just didn't quite know what to do about it.

"What are you doing?" she asked Jules who was standing at her door, a wide-eyed look on his face and waving a limp fist about.

"Umm. Knocking. On your door," he replied.

"Why?"

That's a tough question, thought Jules. Because I want to ask you out? Because I don't understand why we're not friends? Because nothing good has happened since I got back here?

"Me and Dad are over here for a barbecue." Jules decided to keep it simple.

"Oh, right!" said Gen. "Let's just heat up the atmosphere a bit more so we can all stuff our faces with burnt animal." She turned around and walked back into her room. The door was left open so Jules assumed he should follow. "Do you know what that cow's been through? Do you know how much land has been cleared to raise that cow?"

Gen didn't seem to be asking as such, so Jules didn't answer. He just raised his eyebrows in what he hoped was an intelligent way while he half shook and half nodded his head, trying to indicate a possible yes or no. He wasn't all that sure which answer she might have wanted.

"They shoot the cow right in the middle of the head. As it dies, its heart pumps, I don't know, acid and stuff all through its body. You end up eating fear." Gen turned around and stared at him, challenging Jules to respond. Jules thought he'd go with the obvious.

"So, you're vegetarian now?"

"Apart from Big Macs and lamb chops, yes, I am. Pretty much."

Gen laughed and threw herself on the bed, bounced her head off the pillow, and tucked her hands in behind her head.

"Jules Santorini, you big dag. I'm just mucking around. Funny you're back. I never thought I'd see you again."

Oh my God, thought Jules. She's being friendly. That's the old Gen. That's better!

Gen grinned at him and then started singing.

"Julie, Julie, Julie, got a big fat toolie." She started laughing again as she saw the look of horror come across Jules's face.

"Jules! It's OK. Look at you. You're worried I'm going to start singing something from when we were five in the middle of assembly tomorrow. As if. Anyway, you could always sing 'Gen, Gen, Gen, you stink like a hen. If your farts were eggs we'd have a hundred and ten!' "

Jules remembered his own rhyme with painful clarity, but he'd forgotten the one they used to sing about Gen. He started laughing as well and there they were, friends again.

~ Oh, baby, said his brain. We're in. Laughter. Old

times. And we're in the bedroom! Wooowoowoowoowooo!

~ Shut up! said Jules to his brain. Can't you stop thinking about that stuff?

~ Why? You never do.

Sometimes Jules hated his brain. It's true. These days he did seem to think about girls an awful lot of the time, and it managed to be simultaneously fascinating and torturous. But did he have to think about such things right now?

Genevieve Corrigan continued lying on her bed, looking up at the ceiling.

"You were always easy to stir. Remember I told you at school that they could keep you down a class for another year if you got your clothes dirty? You believed that for two days."

Jules did remember that. But he also remembered that whenever they got back here at her place or at his, they could play together for hours and talk a day away. When he left to go and live with his mum, he missed Genevieve more than he missed his dad.

Jules stared at her. Why was it so confusing with her now? He'd been thrilled when she started laughing and talking about them as old friends and then overwhelmed by the sudden burst of emotion in his chest. It actually hurt.

She looked beautiful lying on the bed smiling and trying to remember what came after "big fat toolie." Jules wasn't about to remind her and he turned away.

~ *Think about something else, said his brain. It's not a bad room, huh?*

"Great room," Jules managed to get out, and in fact it was a great room. If you had the syllable "teen" in your age it was the perfect room. The entire roof space of the house had been converted and it was now just a huge open area. There were nooks and crannies everywhere, and on either side of the longer walls there were those windows that stick out of roofs when people put rooms up there giving views to the city on one side and to the mountains on the other. The room was big enough for two beds, an old comfy sofa, a TV, and a big desk with a computer. One wall was painted a warm orange and there were posters and photos pinned up everywhere.

"Bit different to my room," he said. Jules was in the same room he'd had since he was four, and he thought when he got home he would put the toy cars away. Maybe take down the spaceship curtains as well.

"Great posters," said Jules, still facing away from Gen and looking at the movie posters on the wall. It's now or never, he thought. I've got to ask her out or I'm going to go crazy.

~ You're *going to go crazy, said his brain. Do you know what I have to deal with when you get like this?*

"What?" said Gen, who'd been trying to remember the rhyme they made up for their teacher Mrs. Buck back in Year Two.

"Great posters," he repeated, studying them in some detail. "Did you get them at the movies? Umm, you know, Dad says it's OK, now that I'm in Year Eight to go to the movies on my own. You know, with friends and that? Max and some of the guys are going this Friday night. Why don't you and Sonja come too?"

There, he'd done it. He'd asked her out. He was no chicken. Max had said he wouldn't, but he had, so there! He'd asked her out! Forget about Max, he *wanted* to ask her out. Well, no he didn't, he just wanted to be friends again. Well that's what he wanted until he walked in and she started laughing and stuff and well now, yes, he did want to ask her out and he really hoped she'd say yes. . . .

~ *OK, said his brain. Good. Very good. You asked her out. But just calm down on the boyfriend/girlfriend stuff OK, or you are going to blow this very badly.*

Jules felt confident enough to stop studying the movie posters and to turn around and see what Gen's reaction was. That was when he realized that Gen hadn't heard him at all. Or if she had, she was now definitely distracted.

There was someone else in the room.

Someone else who hadn't been in the room when Jules had come into it.

And someone who hadn't come into the room through the door, or even the window. This person hadn't fallen from the sky or crashed through the roof.

This person had just appeared.

Standing between him and Genevieve in the middle of the bedroom was a smallish boy with light chocolatey skin and almond eyes. He seemed a little older than Jules, maybe around fourteen, and Genevieve was staring at him with the kind of incredulous look you can really only achieve when the incredulous actually happens.

And there were plenty of reasons for looking incredulous.

There was the color of this new boy's hair.

Or rather, the colors of his hair.

On the top of his head, his hair was behaving in a way that usually only lights on dance floors behave. It was pulsing colors, changing from red to green to yellow but without in any way resembling a traffic light. It was red for a while, and then bands of green would start to wash through it from the back, growing in intensity until the green won out. The green would then checkerboard with the yellow and then strobe rapidly between the two before the green would become red and then the whole thing would just glow warmly yellow for a moment before the entire sequence began again. Only this time his hair would be green, and bands of red would start to surf down his scalp.

His shoes were purple and fitted him not like shoes, but like a second skin, even outlining his toes. He wore pants of light yellow and a top of blueish green under a long dark coat. In front of him hovered a silver sphere, a little smaller than a basketball.

At first Jules was angry. He'd just asked a girl out for the first time in his life and now it was ruined. Two weeks in the planning. Hours of writing out variations on the invitation. Days spent practicing in front of the bathroom mirror. Should he use the raised eyebrow? The half smile? Head on one side, nodding a little?

His anger lasted about half a second. Then he was disbelieving. The boy, who was now frowning deeply while he pointed what looked like a bright red remote at the silver sphere, had just appeared seemingly out of the air in the middle of Gen's bedroom.

Can't do that, thought Jules. You can't just appear.

Beaming in from hovering spaceships, teleporting from one spot to another, sliding across into alternate universes, none of that's been invented yet, thought Jules.

Happened on TV or in films all the time. In fact, in the

kind of movie that Jules was hoping Gen might accompany him to this coming Friday night, beaming about the universe would be as normal as ducking down to the shop for more cereal as Jules did about twice a week. But Jules felt confident that if the beaming up, down, in, or out of boys about his age was going on in actual Real Life, by now somebody would have mentioned it to him.

Disbelief filled up the last half of the first second after the arrival of the boy with the dance club hair and the hovering sphere. But in the second second after the sudden appearance of the boy with colorful hair, Jules found that he couldn't think about much at all. His brain, which had been so present through the whole stair climbing, door knocking, and asking Gen out episodes had now decided that the sudden materialization of another human being in a bedroom was pretty much impossible and it needed to spend some quiet time alone to think about it. It yelled, THIS CAN'T BE HAPPENING! at Jules and then retreated into its office.

But, despite the protest of Jules's brain, stuff was happening. For example, the boy spoke. He was looking from the remote thing to the sphere thing and around the room and was clearly very puzzled.

"This is it? I win the biggest competition ever, and I end up here? Some girl's bedroom? And it's in Mil 3!" he said in a tone of deep astonishment. "Wurk. Hate Mil 3. Hang on, is that a TV in the corner? Woosh, I could find out what's on! Maybe that's it. I'm here to watch TV!"

The boy took a step or two in the direction of the TV and then stopped.

"Oh, I better not. 'Don't Touch Anything.' These couple of zongoids might think it's a bit weird if the TV suddenly went on."

The boy looked back at Jules and Gen who were frozen with fear and barely blinking or breathing. But they couldn't take their eyes off the boy as he returned to the hovering silver sphere.

"This is not boid. They said it would be totally boid. A JumpSite You'll Never Want To Leave. I want to get out of here now. I mean, Mil 3? Wurk, look at the stuff in this room. And it's so closed in. Waaark!" The boy shook his head and sighed deeply. "I should just go back. I'm sure I'm not meant to be here with the Dodopeople."

The boy looked at Jules and Gen with a sad, unimpressed kind of expression and shook his head. "Frankly, I'd rather sit through a meeting of the Committee for the Invention of the Wheel than hang around with this pair. I mean, look at these two. What is wrong with them? Their eyes keep following me around the room just like those creepy portraits on the Rembrandt Jump."

The boy kept muttering things but Jules couldn't make sense of what he was saying. Partly because it didn't really make sense but more because Jules's eyes and ears kept sending information about the boy to Jules's brain, but his brain was simply refusing to accept it. It just kept telling the eyes and the ears that they were wrong and demanding that they check again.

And obedient little organs that they were, his eyes and ears would check again and then tell his brain for the seven thousandth time that there was a smallish boy, with hair that was putting on a show, wearing a long coat that trailed to the ground, and he was punching buttons on a red remote while shaking his head at a hovering silver sphere.

When his eyes and ears tried to tell his brain for the seven thousandth and first time, Jules's brain just shut the door to its office, hung up an "Out to Lunch" sign, and refused to take any more calls until things had returned to normal.

With his tiny bit of brain that had no choice but to function, Jules did notice that Gen was going through the same thing that he was. Both of them were remaining very still, rigid with the surging adrenaline and fear that was pumping through them. Their eyes were bulging and fixed on the boy in front of them.

And then the boy did something really bizarre.

He started talking to his coat.

"Coat," he said. "It's a little warm in here."

And his coat replied.

"You're right, Theodore. It is a pleasant seventy-five degrees with a slight chance of occasional showers. Full atmospherics coming your way, along with radiation and electromagnetic measures. All part of the service. Can I recommend if you're seeking a faster response, the Deluxe HyperCoat? Truly a prestige garment and always in fashion whatever the Jump—"

"Yip, yip, yip. Thanks, Coat. Believe me, if I could afford a HyperCoat, you wouldn't be here. Why I signed up for PromoCloth, I'll never know. It's just constant ads."

And then Jules's and Gen's eyes bulged even more as the hem of The Coat, which had been brushing the floor, now rose a little above the boy's knees. The very weave of the fabric opened up a little and The Coat's sleeves unbuttoned and rolled themselves up to the middle of his forearm.

Wardrobe adjusted, the boy who seemed to be named Theodore turned his attention to Jules and Gen. He walked around them, examining their clothes.

"What is this boy wearing?" he said. "Why does he need all those pockets on his pants? And you wouldn't catch me in that shirt. She looks a bit better, but I bet you they have to wear the same clothes all day. Geesh, that'd be dull." The boy looked back and forth between the two of them and he shook his head with weary puzzlement.

"No wonder we never come to Mil 3. Look at this pair. The boy's dribbling and the girl looks like she's seen a . . ."

Theodore stopped and stood as still as Jules and Gen.

Then he took a step backward.

Jules and Gen didn't take their eyes off him.

Theodore took a few steps forward and as he watched them watch him, a look of horror came over his face. His hair slowed right down and went the kind of green hair goes when it's spent the afternoon in a heavily chlorinated pool. It looked ghastly with his skin tones.

"Oh my DNA," he whispered. "I'm present!"

And then he leapt forward at Gen, who screamed and tried to retreat to the other side of her bed. He turned around to Jules who backed away defensively.

"No, no, *no*!" shouted Theodore. "I can't be present. This is, this is . . ."

But whatever this was remained a mystery. Theodore collapsed weakly onto the sofa, his head down in his hands, his fingers rubbing at his eyes. Once or twice he looked up at Jules and Gen and moaned, as though he were in pain.

"Mil 3. With Dodopeople. Visible in Mil 3. This can't be it. I mean, they said a big prize, and this can't be it."

The silver sphere had followed him and was now hovering sympathetically near his left shoulder. He chewed on the red remote and his hair made occasional limp attempts to get started again but it seemed to lack the spirit. The Coat spoke up.

"Atmosphere Report, Theodore, brought to you by Real-Fish, So Real You'll Think It Swam Over For Dinner! It's 74.84 degrees, barometer rising, and it looks like a pleasant day ahead. You're in the early evening, local time is around 7:15 p.m. Occasional showers expected along the coast but overall—"

"Shut up," ordered Theodore. "Shut up shut up shut up shut up," he kept on repeating a little hysterically. "You are as useless as a moontan. A real Coat might be of some actual help here. I mean, have you noticed that we're visible?"

"Oh, is *that* what it is? I *thought* there was a particle anomaly. Are you sure you're looking your best? New Molecule Follicle Gel makes your hair—"

"Shut up!"

The Coat fell silent.

Everyone fell silent.

Jules sat down on a chair.

Gen sat forward on the edge of her bed.

Theodore sucked at the remote in a worried kind of way.

A tiny sound escaped from Gen. Her lips moved, but only the faintest whisper came out.

Theodore looked at her with a nervous expression on his face. "Did you speak?" he asked.

Gen nodded and in a voice a little louder than a baby's whimper she asked, "Who are you?"

Jules was impressed. He had enough brain power for sitting down, maybe scratching an armpit, but not much else. Gen had managed a question. Her brain obviously wasn't hiding under a blanket in a back room.

"You talk?" Theodore seemed surprised. He looked at Jules.

"You talk too? I mean, normally. You know Speakish?"

Jules sent out the directions for his head to nod but he wasn't really sure if they got there or not.

"Umm, yeah, English. What you're talking. We call it English," said Gen.

Theodore leaned forward a bit with an alert look on his face.

"English? And what was that first thing you said? Yarr? Yey? Yee? Yair? Coat, what'd she say?"

"Thanks for asking, Theo. Yeah is the equivalent of your 'yip,'" said The Coat helpfully. "She also referred to English, which is the root language of Speakish. You want me to run a TalkCheck on anything else? Remember, I'm loaded with AllTalk. Getting No Action on a Word? You need AllTalk—No Action, All Talk—"

"Yip, yip, thanks Coat, that'll do. Huh, well, we can talk then." And Theodore smiled a bit, although nothing about his manner suggested that he was in any way happy.

"Not that there's much we can talk about. There's nothing I can tell you," he continued.

"What?" asked Gen, a little louder than before. "Nothing you can tell us about what?"

"About anything. I can tell you nothing about everything. I can't tell you anything."

"Why not?"

"Well, I can't tell you why I can't tell you. That'd be the same as telling you."

"Telling us what?"

"Anything."

"I haven't asked anything yet," said Gen, getting a little louder with each statement.

"No, but you're going to and I'm just saying I won't be able to tell you anything."

"Can you tell us why your hair was amazing when you got here and now it looks like snot?" asked Gen innocently.

"What? Where's a mirror?" Theodore leapt up and scuttled around the room, the sphere flashing after him. He found Gen's dressing table and peered in.

"Wurk! Thank my lucky genomes no one saw it like this! Must have been the shock. What's snot, anyway?" he asked as he did a little dance in front of the mirror and his hair leapt back into action, reds, greens, and yellows forming little spirals all over his head.

"You know, snot. I don't know what it is," said Gen starting to feel a bit annoyed at this intruder. She wasn't enjoying this. She was terrified at his sudden appearance, and now he was being annoying. Not that Theodore seemed to care. He was too busy dancing in front of the mirror and getting his hair to do tricks.

"There! That's it. Totally boid, eh?"

"Totally what?"

"You know, boid? Not unboid."

"How do you get to do that?" asked Gen.

Theodore stopped dancing around and got serious again.

"Nip. Love to tell you all about it. But I can't. Sorry."

"I don't get this," said Gen. "You've just landed in my room, you're going on about all this stuff, and you won't tell us anything. Why not, *Theodore*?"

Theodore looked astonished.

"How do you know my name?" he asked.

"It's what your Coat calls you. Should I bother asking where you get a talking coat?"

Jules was very impressed. He'd gone to speak a couple of times but he'd been staring at Theodore for so long with his mouth open that his tongue was drowning in a small lake of drool. He'd swallowed it, nearly choked, and was only just starting to recover. His brain, too, was beginning to take an interest again. It had come over to its office door and was peeking around the blind. But Jules had to admit that Gen and her brain were doing fine. She was getting very tetchy at this kid and starting to have a go at him, and the boy, Theodore, was looking very uncomfortable.

"Look," Theodore was saying, starting to sound exasperated, "what's so hard to understand here? I tell you anything, I'm telling you everything. It's for your own good."

"Our own good?" Gen was back to full volume. "You beam in here and then start acting like my mother?"

"Look, I'm sorry. This is all very hard for me, too. Do you know what I just won—look, I can't say, but believe me, you can't be the prize."

"Thanks. That's really nice." Gen flung herself down on the sofa, folded her arms, and huffed angrily for a while.

"Can't you even tell us where you came from? Are you from another planet?" asked Jules, deciding he better join in. He didn't like the way Gen and Theodore were sparring. The way they were fighting they'd be friends in another five minutes and then where would he be?

"We on Earth?" asked Theodore.

"Yes," replied Jules.

"Then no, I'm not from another *planet*," Theodore answered carefully.

"What's Mil 3?" Jules asked.

"Don't you know?" asked Theodore.

"No. That's why I'm asking."

"Then I can't tell you."

"He's great to talk to, isn't he Jules?" said Gen. "So glad you dropped in, Theodore. Anytime you got nothing to say, come on over."

Jules thought he might keep trying the noninflammatory approach.

"So you're sure there's nothing you can tell us? You can't tell us where you're from, how you got here, anything?"

"Well, I can tell you that this can't be happening," Theodore offered.

"What can't be happening?"

"This. Me. Here. You two. Us. Can't be happening."

"It is happening."

"Hmmm. But if it *was* really happening then it would have happened already."

"When?"

"When what?"

"When would it have happened already?"

"Before."

"Before what?"

"Well, before I got here."

"How could it have happened *before* you got here? It didn't start happening *until* you got here."

"Well that's just how it seems to you."

Jules thought he understood more when Theodore wasn't telling him anything.

"But look, I'm sorry, I really can't say anything. I've said too much already."

Theodore's Coat spoke up. "Having trouble with the whole Time–Space thing? Can I recommend *TimeJumping For Dummies*? It's a great new publication written by the only six people on the Two Planets who really understand how TimeMaster JumpMan and JumpMan Pro really work. TimeJumping, it's incomprehensible really, but you'll think you understand with *TimeJumping For Dummies*, just $19.95 at your nearest TimeMaster Dealer. Theodore, you really should eat."

Theodore sat there trying to look like his Coat had just gone mad. Jules's mouth fell open. Gen sat up on her bed, a slow smile creeping across her face.

"Would you, by chance, be from another *time*?" she asked sweetly.

Theodore cracked a little. There was just the tiniest

tremble in his bottom lip. His eyes darted back and forth, his breath went shallow, and for a moment his hair was the brightest red possible.

"I can't tell you. And I've really got to go. I think I was meant to be back about ten minutes ago."

Gen shook her head, a puzzled grin on her face.

"Well, go then. But if you're staying any longer I think you have to tell us what's going on here."

Theodore paced around the room. He aimed the remote at the sphere and it settled down on one of the beds.

"This is all wrong," he said, nervously rubbing his hands together. "I'm not meant to be present. No one is. It's the Code. Only one rule when you TimeJump: Don't Touch Anything. I've already broken it by being visible and this Coat's in real trouble for spilling the lentils like that."

"Spilling the lentils?" asked Gen.

"Yip. You know, spilling the lentils. Letting the armadillo out of the trunk."

Gen figured it out.

"We spill the beans and let the cat out of the bag."

"What's a cat?" asked Theodore.

"You don't have cats?" said Jules.

"No. They must have all gone when—" Theodore stopped himself, shaking his head as if to tell himself off for talking too much. "Anyway, telling you stuff about where or when I'm from . . . it's just wrong. It's interfering with history. You two now know about TimeTravel, and that's not meant to happen. Unless it is meant to happen. In which case it would have already happened, and I'd know about it."

Theodore looked at them.

"See? You don't understand a single thing I'm saying, right? Oh my twisted helix, a Bone Box, and it's working. You gotta tell me what you do with that thing." Theodore was pointing at Gen's computer.

"Why?" she demanded. "You won't tell us anything. Why do we have to tell you what my computer does?"

"*That's* a computer?" Theodore leapt on it.

Jules was amazed at Gen's capacity to banter with this guy. He was still reeling from the talking Coat and its statement about time travel. He'd like to read *TimeJumping For Dummies* and then maybe banter a little. Gen was simply annoyed at Theodore's refusal to answer anything. Even though she was arguing with him, she was still scared of him. She also wasn't quite sure how to explain Theodore to her mother.

"But it's enormous!" said Theodore.

The Coat spoke again. "Please stand by for a Nutritional Monitoring Update, brought to you by the new Tempo Bar. Theo, right now, NM indicates that in all major food groups you are running at low," said his Coat. "When you get in the red, be like the top TimeJumpers and bite into the new Tempo Bar. It's got minerals, vitamins, proteins, carbohydrates, and it tastes yummy too. Everything to keep your particles partying whenever they might be—"

"Let's get the computer to deal with that. Computer, I need a Tempo Bar or something that contains around twenty-five per cent protein, some assorted minerals and vitamins, and I'll need around one hundred and fifty grams of it. Go easy on the unsaturated fats, all right? Thank you."

The computer sat there and Gen's screen saver, which was a collage she'd made herself by clicking and dragging everything she could find on DJ Thurston Howl, her current favorite musician, rolled about like screen savers do. It didn't suddenly produce a peanut let alone a Tempo Bar.

"Hmmm. It's not working. What's a Qwertyuiop?" asked Theodore.

"A what?" said Gen.

"This flat thing in front of your computer. It says 'Qwertyuiop' right here, and then it says 'Asdfghjkl.' I don't know how you'd say that," Theodore replied.

"Oh," said Gen. "That's the keyboard. That's how we work the computer. Or you can use a mouse."

"You've got mice that operate computers?"

"No, just what we call this thing here," said Gen, pointing

at the mouse and then clicking on DJ Thurston Howl's hair for a full list of his favorite shampoos.

"Wow. That is such hard work. Coat, can you believe this computer thing?"

"Theodore, what you're looking at there was once known as a Personal Computer."

"It's about as personal as a fridge." Theodore snorted.

"For real computing power," continued The Coat, "grow your OrganoNanos in Silica Soil. Each Nanobot reaches ultimate computing threshold—"

"Shut up, Coat," ordered Theodore, and The Coat subsided, although a small screen did fold out from its right lapel and continue to relay information about Theodore's blood flow, oxygen levels, and nutritional requirements.

Theodore turned around and smiled at them.

"Oak eye," said Theodore, or at least that's what it sounded like to Jules. "Look, I'm really sorry. This is a really big mistake. I have just won the biggest competition and, well, something's gone wrong. You can't pay us to come to Mil 3, let alone expect to sell the new JumpMan by offering it as a prize. Anyway, much as I would love to stay and see what you did with those Bone Boxes, and I'm dying to find out what was on TV . . . We've found millions of them, but when we turn them on there's nothing to watch. But another time, so to speak. Like I said, this really wasn't meant to happen, so I'm going to get going and sort a few things out. There'll be a Code Cop here in a day or two, and after that you won't even remember this. And even if no one drops by to clean up, in a little while you'll think you dreamed the whole thing. It makes no sense, does it? So, if it's oak eye with you, I'll be out of here. Sonee haha."

Jules gathered that last bit meant "good-bye," as Theodore gave them a cheery wave. His Coat extended back to the dramatic full length it had been when he'd arrived, his hair went into an extraordinary performance, strobing purple spots on a red background. He aimed the remote at the hovering sphere, closed his eyes, and pushed the large black button on the front of the remote.

Nothing happened.

Theodore opened his eyes.

Jules raised his eyebrows, and Gen looked a little condescendingly at him.

"Ummm," said Theodore as the bedroom door opened and in walked Gen's parents, her little sister, and Jules's dad.

Katherine Corrigan had knocked and then came in first, calling out, "Hellooo. It's just us." Katherine was a little highly strung at the best of times. She had a stressful job as a shift manager in a call center. She'd finish work at four in the afternoon and then pick up her younger daughter, Cynthia, and then organize the house. She was easily rattled and tended to expect disaster in most situations, but when relaxed she was cheerful. As she walked into Gen's bedroom, she felt that the day's toil was behind her, and by the time she'd finished the glass of red wine in her hand she'd probably be feeling pretty good.

But then she caught sight of Theodore.

Or more exactly, she caught sight of Theodore disappearing.

As the door opened, Theodore had glimpsed the adults on their way in. Gen and Jules had both swung around to see what was happening and partly hidden him from the parents coming in through the door. Theodore had punched a button on the remote and, unlike his previous attempt, this one had worked.

In the same kind of astonishingly instantaneous manner in which he'd suddenly appeared in the room, he vanished.

Katherine, coming through the doorway first, had seen a third person in the room. And by the time she'd got over her surprise—the third person did seem to have red and purple hair—the third person had vanished.

"Gen! Who was . . . ? Was there someone else . . . ?" Katherine was having trouble finishing her sentences. "Did someone just . . . ?"

Gen looked around her room and then at her mother, her eyes wide with mystified innocence.

"What, Mum? Someone else, what?"

"I'm sure I saw someone else here when we . . ." Katherine was beginning to wonder what she was talking about.

"What are you going on about, Kat?" asked Steven Corrigan, Gen's dad, coming in behind her.

"Oh this is great! Nice job, Steven. You did all this yourself?" Tony Santorini, Jules's dad, brought up the rear. Scuttling between them was seven-year-old Cynthia, her eyes darting everywhere.

"G'day, Gen," said Tony. "Sorry to barge in, but Steven just had to show off. Not bad for an accountant, mate."

"Fully square and under budget," said Steven proudly.

"How much do you love this room, Gen?" asked Tony.

"Yeah, it's pretty good, Mr. Santorini."

"Oh, call me Tony. Come on, you've got your own room, you're in Year Eight. It's Tony, OK?"

"Sure, Mr. . . . umm, Tony."

Tony walked around inspecting the renovations. He was a site manager on big building projects in town. But in his own house, he couldn't put up bookshelves that were straight. Katherine walked around the room as well, peering under the desk and opening all the cupboards. Steven remained in the doorway, showing off his handiwork to Tony but also trying to figure out what his wife was up to.

"You looking for something, Kat?" he asked.

"Yes," she replied. "No. I don't know."

"OK," said Steven.

Jules and Gen didn't dare look at each other. They were both feeling a bit weak and faint. First they'd been rigid with fear and tension and then totally confused by Theodore. It was a lot to have happen in half an hour and now having the entire family in the room on a kind of inspection wasn't helping them at all. They were both pale, and Jules had quietly collapsed on the sofa while Gen had sat down on her bed. Cynthia watched them both. There was something going on, she just knew it.

"I've been doing a bit of reading," said Tony as he looked out at the view, "and they say you've got to be a bit careful about the 'teen retreat.' Particularly with boys. You put 'em in something like this too early, they brood. Grow away from you. You never know what's going on." Tony Santorini loved his son and loved having Jules back living with him, but he couldn't help noticing that every day in the newspaper there seemed to be something about how badly boys were doing these days. He worried about it and read a lot of books on the topic.

"What's that, Tony?" asked Steven, looking away from Katherine who had now turned on every light in the room.

"You know. Good for girls, this sort of setup. They've got that maturity," said Tony.

"Yeah," Steven replied, not really listening. He was a bit disappointed with Tony's reaction. He worked as an accountant by day and was very proud of the work he did around the place at night and on the weekends. Putting in this room had been his biggest project ever. Tony was going on like this kind of place was some sort of problem. And what on Earth was wrong with Katherine?

"Anyway, there it is," he said. "Months of precision handiwork done by a master. Thank you for your unstinting praise. Shall we go and eat?"

Steven led Tony out the door, possibly to get his attention away from Katherine who was backing out of the room without taking her eyes off Gen and Jules.

When she got to the door, she stopped. "Dinner. It's ready. Come. You two." She was still having difficulty forming complete sentences but she remembered there was more red wine downstairs and a barbecue and decided that she better get back to it as quickly as possible.

Jules and Gen got up, still without looking at each other, and followed their parents out of the room.

chapter two

Time Will Tell

Dinner was awful.

It felt to Jules like they'd been sitting around the table for several weeks. See? Here it is again, he thought. We're all having a lousy time and it feels like it's taking forever. It feels like time is sulking in a corner somewhere and every now and again it gets up grumpily and hauls another second out of the way.

It's the wrong way around, he thought. When you're having the time of your life, time should slow right down, so you can enjoy it for longer. And when things are awful, like sitting at this dinner table watching everyone squabble, time should skip by so you don't have to suffer.

~ I really want you to stop this kind of thinking, said his brain. I don' t know about you, but I' m exhausted.

So was Jules. He looked across at Gen and could see she was feeling the same. The half hour with Theodore had completely drained them and they were in a kind of state of mild shock. And now, sitting here at dinner, they had to work hard at appearing normal. It was pretty tough. They couldn't stop staring at each other, as if by meeting each other's eyes they could reassure each other that everything that had just happened had just happened. And Gen's mother wanted the truth.

Katherine had come downstairs, slammed dinner down in front of everyone, quickly drunk two glasses of red wine, and was now ignoring her food and slurping down a third.

"I'm sorry, Steven," she was saying as Jules tuned in again. "But I know what I saw so I am going to ask the question again. Genevieve, who was that in your room?"

Steven groaned. Tony looked extremely uncomfortable and only Cynthia seemed to be enjoying the proceedings. Gen took a deep breath and looked her mother right in the eye.

"Mum! There was no one else in the room. How could there be? If there was someone else in the room, they'd be here now, eating burnt chops with us, OK?"

"Don't get smart with me, young girl! I know how sneaky kids can be. I don't know how you did it, but someone was there and they disappeared. Just tell us who it was and how they're coming and going, and you won't hear another word from me."

"Mum, there's nothing else I can tell you, except there wasn't anyone there."

Gen's face crumpled a little and she pushed her plate away and then sat there staring down at it.

"Come on, Katherine. No one else saw anything."

"Steven! You always take her side. Are you saying I'm seeing things?"

"No, of course not. But no one else saw it, OK?" Steven was getting angry. He could see where this was going. Katherine had wanted the room upstairs to be a parents' retreat, not teenage heaven.

"Steven, you know what I think. It's like Tony was saying. They get a room like that, and who knows what starts going on." Katherine finished her wine and started to circle the table clearing up plates that weren't really finished yet. No one felt like stopping her.

Except for Gen, who kept her head down and hung on to her plate as Katherine tried to take it away. After a brief struggle, Katherine let out an angry snort and stomped off to the kitchen with the rest of the plates. Gen pushed her food around a bit and then, still with her head down, lifted her eyes and caught Jules's gaze.

Jules felt a tremor run up his spine. Gen's eyes were bright with tears. What did this look mean? He felt he should look away, but then what would she think? But if he kept on staring at her was that any better? Is she sending out a mute appeal for help? Is she sending out sympathetic thought beams that say "We've been through so much together tonight, and by the way, I'd love to come to the movies with you this Friday?" Or is she thinking, "Do something, you useless lump. Get us out of here. Otherwise I'd rather go to the movies with a piece of dog poo on my shoe than go with you." It was hard to tell.

He felt he'd better break this locked gaze before anyone else noticed.

"Jules loves Ge-en. Jules loves Ge-en."

Too late. Gen's little sister had seen it all, of course.

Seven years old and at the height of her powers, Cynthia sat back and watched her family. She was the youngest, but this was her strength. She could sit there quietly and everyone would forget she was there. They'd start talking and she'd hear everything. Her sweet exterior hid a hungry curiosity that was focused entirely on the other three members of her family and a nagging anxiety that there was something they weren't telling her. She must find out! Her parents and her sister still regarded her as a little girl, too little to understand what they were saying. Unbeknown to them she took everything in, storing it in fresh eager memory banks, ready for the day when it could be used to her advantage. Cynthia was like an undercover agent. When it seemed she was sitting on the floor playing with Gen's old Barbies, she was in fact all ears and all eyes, soaking up the mysterious actions of her parents and her sister and watching for that vital clue so that finally she would understand what was going on. Then she, too, would be allowed to grow up.

In the meantime, while she watched and waited, she was happy to manipulate her family. If there was a little tension in the house, she would sense it and then poke at it to provoke it further. If there was a secret being kept, she'd smell the air of secrecy and track it to its source. A tiny chink of vulnerability or emotion and she'd worry at it like an itchy dog until it burst open for everyone to see.

Gen knew how dangerous Cynthia was, and so she was doing everything she could to appear normal. She hoped she was giving off a firm impression that she hadn't just been arguing with a boy with technicolor hair from the future who'd just up and disappeared again. She wondered why she was having trouble eating her dinner and then she noticed that she was trying to cut off a piece of barbecued chop with her spoon. She tried to discreetly put it down and equally discreetly pick up her knife.

"Jules loves Ge-en," sang Cynthia. "And Gen's eating her chop with her spo-oon." Of course Cynthia had noticed. And of course she made sure everyone else did as well by laughing her evil laugh, a manic cackle that sounded real to the rest of the family but that Gen knew was about as real as chewing gum teeth.

Cynthia was in her element. Everything had been normal before they went upstairs, but now the adults were bickering and Jules and Gen looked completely freaked out. This was great! Just keep watch, she thought, and soon she would know exactly what had happened up there in Gen's room. She cackled again, this time with genuine delight.

"Yes, all right, Cynthia. That'll do," Steven ordered, but he looked from Gen to Jules with mild amusement.

Jules's dad opened his mouth to speak, shut it, opened it again, and then paused somewhere between open and shut. He looked like a dying trout. He had a slightly pained expression around his eyes. They're just kids, he wanted to say, but then, Jules is over thirteen and Gen's nearly fourteen. I guess they're not just kids. And then he wanted to say something about boyfriends and girlfriends, first love and all that kind of stuff, and whatever he thought of sounded like a bad greeting card and he suspected that if he said it, Jules would never talk to him again about anything except breakfast cereal and money. The articles and books he'd been reading were right. Raising boys was hard. At least as hard as raising girls.

Jules was thankful for his father's silence. He tried not to look at Gen. Or Cynthia. Or Steven, or Katherine, or his father for that matter. And so he was now staring off to the side of the door, trying to look like he was interested in the light switches. In reality he was again experiencing that sinking feeling that he'd made a terrible mistake coming back here.

He'd been away living with his mum and her new boyfriend for only two years. It hadn't seemed that long, until he got back here. Now it seemed like he must have been away for a couple of centuries.

So much had changed. This dinner, for example. When his mum and his dad and he lived up the road and the two families were like one family, dinners together used to be so much fun. Tonight it was like eating with cousins you can't stand.

~ *Well, are you going to do something? asked his brain.*

~ *Oh thanks, brain. You were so much use upstairs when you went off and hid, and now you're back and all you can do is demand things.*

~ *Time to decide. You can't just crawl off home. Do that*

and she'll never forgive you. You'll never know if she wanted to go out with you or not.

As usual, Jules's brain was right. He wanted to stand up and say he had a lot of homework and then sneak off home. And then when he got there, he wanted to hide in his bed and secretly suck his thumb for a while. But then he desperately wanted to get back upstairs to see if Theodore had come back.

~ He's gone.

~ You didn't even think he was there in the first place, said Jules.

~ Hey, leave me alone. Do you know how many brain cells I had to argue with when that kid turned up?

~ So you believe it now?

~ Maybe.

"Dessert! Jules, do you want dessert?"

Jules had to stop arguing with his brain because Katherine was asking him something. He noticed that things were very quiet around the table. He wondered if he'd been talking with his brain for too long. But then he realized it was nothing to do with him.

Katherine was serving dessert. She had her apron on back to front and she was standing at the table putting scoops of ice cream into the salad. Next to the salad bowl was a bowl of fruit salad, but Katherine didn't appear to be aware that she'd picked up the wrong bowl. Instead she was starting in on Gen again as she mixed the ice cream in with the salad and then spooned it out into their bowls.

"I'm locking that room up," she declared. "You can go back and share with Cynthia."

"Mum!" Gen wailed.

"Katherine! I didn't spend a year building that room to have it locked up!" yelled Steven angrily.

"Mrs. Corrigan?" Jules spoke up and everyone went silent. They all looked at him.

"Umm, perhaps you should talk about this without us. Could we take our dessert upstairs and then you could come and tell us what you've decided?"

Katherine's eyes narrowed. "No! I'm not going to have you two—"

"Just go!" yelled Steven. "Go on, up you go. Perfectly good idea, Jules, thank you."

"They are not going up there—"

"Katherine! We'll talk about this in a moment. The kids are going up there to eat their dessert and do homework. They are not contacting aliens who pop up in their room or whatever it is you think is going on up there."

This was a bit close to the truth for Jules but he kept heading for the stairs behind Genevieve who was already halfway up.

"Me too!" piped Cynthia. "You can't talk about all this in front of me either!"

"No! It's Gen's room. If she wants you to go up, she'll ask you to go up," said Steven.

Gen didn't and the next sound they heard was her door slamming, followed by Jules opening it and then closing it a little more gently.

"OK. The TV's all yours, Cynthia. Katherine, sit down. Have you forgotten Tony's here?"

Katherine sat down noisily at the end of the table and then mumbled, "Sorry, Tony. Bit stressed."

"Sure, Kath," said Tony.

Instead of talking about anything the three adults sat there in moody silence, each casting around for something to say that wouldn't start a fight again. They poked at their desserts, except for Katherine, who ate a little and then stopped. She pulled a piece of lettuce out of her teeth, and finally noticed the full bowl of fruit salad. She looked across the table at the two men looking at her and they all started to laugh.

Theodore was back.

He was sitting on Gen's bed when they came in. The

sphere was hovering around him and he was poking at buttons on the remote. His hair was striping red and green in a relaxed kind of way.

"Why didn't this JumpMan do an abort? It should have detected particles shifting into present—oh hello, is that food?"

He leapt up and grabbed the bowl out of Gen's hand.

"What's that?" he asked peering down at it.

"Salad," said Gen. "And ice cream."

Theodore started eating.

"Oh my giddy clone, what did you say this was?"

"Ice cream."

"And this is what you put on salads? It's fantastic! Mmmmmmm."

Jules and Gen exchanged a look as Theodore's Coat sprang into action. The screen on the right lapel lit up and text, charts, and graphs started to scroll across it.

"Theo! Foodstuffs just consumed do not meet International Food Conference Standards. Faint traces of dairy product, but as for the rest, I'll have to work on it for a while. Are you sure you're meant to be eating this? It's not a cleaning agent of some kind?"

"Coat! You've got no taste, that's obvious!"

"Theo. Eddie. You've got to listen to me. Whatever you're eating could be dangerous! You must eat properly and eat properly soon. Have you tried the new Yummy Tummy Tofu Bite? It's light on the bite and—"

"Shut up, Coat."

The Coat subsided but continued to send analyses of the salad and ice cream across its screen.

"Ice cream, is that what you said?" checked Theodore. "Mmmm, this stuff is oak eye. Totally boid. I gotta take this stuff back. What's in it?"

"I don't know," said Gen, wearily slumping down onto the sofa.

"You don't know? You eat stuff and you don't know what it is?" Theodore looked amazed.

"No, I just mean, I don't know right now. It's ice. And cream. And probably lots of other stuff that gives you cancer. I don't know." Gen sounded tired and a bit distraught after arguing with her mother.

"You guys eat weird stuff. I found a Tempo Bar and it tasted disgusting."

Theodore held up a half-chewed lipstick of Gen's.

"That's my new Avarice. It's not food!"

"I'll say it's not. It's awful. Looks just like a Tempo Bar, though."

Gen got up angrily from the sofa and snatched the half-eaten lipstick from Theodore and threw it back on her dressing table.

"You've never eaten ice cream?" asked Jules, trying to lighten the mood a little. He was excited to see Theodore again. Theodore's hair was now spiraling yellow on black, The Coat was flashing up further information about the ice cream and was trying to tell Theodore to eat more of the green leafy bits, and the sphere was hovering just near his elbow.

"I've never eaten anything like this. This is the *best* salad dressing ever. You going to eat yours?"

"No, no please . . ." began Jules.

Theodore grabbed the plate from Jules and quickly scoffed it down. Finished eating, he sat back on the bed and stuck out his feet. His shoes opened up down the middle and fell to the floor. He picked up the remote, pulled a sour face, and poked at it a little more.

~ He's back again, said Jules's brain.

~ Yes, he is. Do you believe it now?

~ Him coming and going, it's starting to seem normal.

Gen stretched out on the sofa and looked at Theodore for a bit, who was now closely examining his JumpMan.

"You came back," she said in a flat kind of voice.

"Uh-huh," said Theodore, preoccupied with the remote.

"Where did you go?"

"Oh, I did a JumpOut . . . Look, we've been through this before. I can't tell you anything, oak eye?"

"Well, just go then!" yelled Gen. "And it's OK, not oak eye! Go on, go. You're getting me into trouble and I don't care if you're from tomorrow or a million years in the future. Just go!"

Jules felt a surge of happiness. Maybe this Theodore guy could disappear again, never come back, and he could find out if Gen wanted to go out with him on Friday. But then he felt a surge of disappointment. There was something exciting about having a guy with dancefloor hair and a talking coat from another time hanging around. In fact, he felt good enough to risk a question.

"So, you're from the future, right?" asked Jules.

"No, I'm from the past," answered Theodore sarcastically. "In the days of Robin Hood, they actually had really big computers and they used them to program bows and arrows. What do you reckon, zongoid?" Theodore looked at him like he was a disease. Being yelled at by Gen had obviously turned off the chirpy Theodore. His hair had turned a stark white with three sharp Vs along the crown. Jules decided he just wanted him to go.

"Sorry for asking. You don't have to be a jerk about it," said Jules.

"A what? I don't have to be a what?" Theodore looked up from the remote.

"A jerk. A pain. We're just trying to help."

"Yeah, well, thanks, but I don't think a real toenail like yourself can do much, all right?" Things were turning ugly.

"A 'toenail'?" said Jules. "Is that your worst?"

"No. But I'm not going to hang around moron Mil 3 long enough to get really nasty, oh kay?" Theodore pronounced each letter carefully and sarcastically. "I mean, look at you. Is that all you're ever going to do with your hair? Did you choose that shirt or did your mummy program it for you? You're an applesticker, a moondrone. You are clonecrap, you know that? Whenever. I'm gone. I'm Jumped. I'm not going to waste any more time in this time wasting time on you."

Theodore turned his back on them and started furiously punching buttons on the remote.

Jules looked at Gen. She shook her head in disbelief. The two of them closed in on Theodore.

"Well?" said Gen.

"Well, what?" said Theodore.

"You going?"

"Probably," said Theo.

"Well, bye then," said Jules.

Theodore looked from one to the other as they stood over him glaring at him.

"I can't," he confessed.

"Can't what?" asked Gen.

"Go."

"You're stuck here, aren't you?" said Gen.

"For a little while."

"You need our help, don't you?" said Jules.

"Maybe." Theodore was looking uncomfortable and was retreating from them, down the bed.

"Well, you're going to have to talk to us, or we can't help you." Gen folded her arms and looked witheringly at Theodore.

Theodore withered. He fell back on the bed and moaned. "This is very bad. Unboid to the red. Beyond the red. Should I just Jump back? But what if it goes wrong? Plus it doesn't seem to want to do it. Ooooohhhh."

He curled up into a small ball and moaned for a bit longer. Jules wasn't sure whether this was some kind of trick and in two seconds more he'd be snarling at him again and calling him a toenail or belly fluff or something. He and Gen just watched and waited. Theodore mumbled into his arms.

"Coat, are you recording all this?"

"Of course, up to twelve hours instant recall of all action is available on demand. To save the previous twelve hours, just say 'Save.' Of course, you can record it all with total surround sound in new DeepPan DublyX just by ordering—"

"Shut up, Coat," ordered Theodore.

Theodore thought for a while.

"Save," he ordered.

"Sure thing, Eddie," said The Coat.

Theodore sighed, took a deep breath, sat up, and grinned at them both.

"Hi! How are you?" he said cheerily. "I'm Theodore Pine Four, to use my full title. Theo, Ed, Eddie, Needle, to use some of my many budhandles and I'm from the year Fifteen Billion and Seventy-three. Who are you chicks?"

"You're from *when*?" burst out Jules.

"Please! Introductions first," said Theodore.

"I . . . I'm Jules Santorini and this is Genevieve Corrigan. Did you say, Fifteen Billion and—"

"Seventy-three," said Theodore.

"When is that?" asked Jules. It felt like a very stupid question and Theodore looked at him like he'd asked a very stupid question.

"When is that?" he mimicked. "What kind of question is that? It's just after Fifteen Billion and Seventy-two and little before Fifteen Billion and Seventy-four. When do you think it is?"

"You're from *billions* of years in the future?" exclaimed Gen.

"Oh, right," said Theodore. "Of course, you guys are on Old Time. This is Mil 3, right? Early third millennium Old Time. We're on All Time. We measure time from the Big Bang. All Time," explained Theodore brightly.

Jules and Gen nodded. Jules tried to get his brain to keep up, but his brain was backing away again and just kept saying, "Huh?"

"So, Fifteen Billion and Seventy-three is about three thousand years in the future. Give or take a century. The conversions are a bit tricky. What is it exactly, Coat?"

"Three thousand, one hundred and ninety-eight years, Theo, and that Time Conversion was brought to you by TimeMaster, the makers of JumpMan and JumpMan Pro, and all your TimeJumping accessories. TimeMaster: For When You've Got All The Time In The World."

"Sorry about that," said Theodore. "I'm saving up for a real Coat. You can get PromoCloth free, but the ads drive you crazy."

"Why do you measure time from the Big Bang?" asked Jules, sure that this was probably another stupid question but desperate to know more.

"Well, you have to," said Theodore. "Can't TimeJump if you don't know when you're going. You could end up anywhen, and that could be somewhen you don't want to be."

Theodore's language makes sense, thought Jules, if you don't try to understand what he's saying.

"You know about the Big Bang, right?" Theodore continued. "It's where and when the universe started. Before Big Bang, everything in the universe is packed up in this tiny box. After the Big Bang, everything is out of the box and starts racing all over the place. Because now there's space for everything to race. And there's time as well." Theodore was smiling at them as though he was just reminding them of how to count to ten.

"So the big discovery for us was exactly when the Big Bang happened. Not sort of, not a guess, but exactly. We discovered that, let me see, back in Fourteen Billion, Nine Hundred and Ninety-nine Million, Nine Hundred and Ninety-nine Thousand, Nine Hundred and Seventy-five. What a great year that was." Theodore looked dreamy.

"Well, that's what our parents say, anyway," he continued. "It was the year of Return. Theodore Pine One came back to Earth that first year. Anyway, once we knew exactly when the Big Bang had happened, TimeJumping became relatively simple. You just have to sort out when you are and then away you can go. Oddly enough, it's proved much easier than space travel."

Jules managed to add things up.

"So you're from about Five Thousand, One Hundred and Ninety-three or something, in our time. Old Time."

"Yeah, something like that."

"Are you the only kid time jumping or whatever it is?" asked Gen.

"Nip. Every kid's got one," said Theodore. "Most popular

thing since SolarBlades. Killed Gene Swapping. Come the weekend, no one's home. Kids are anywhen from the Big Bang to yesterday."

Jules and Gen were now sitting on the floor in front of Gen's bed. Theodore was sitting up on her bed looking very chirpy. His hair was grooving away happily, the sphere was hovering just above Gen's doona, and The Coat was still analysing Theo's recent food intake. It was having trouble reconciling Theo's level of food satisfaction with the total absence of any actual food, apart from a couple of lettuce leaves.

"So what's wrong?" asked Gen. "Is that thing a JumpMan?" She pointed at the sphere. "How come you're stuck?"

"This," said Theodore, grabbing the sphere out of the air, "is not just a JumpMan. This is a brand-new TimeMaster JumpMan Pro. I just won a two-planet-wide competition to be the first kid to use it. It's got ten to the power twenty-five OrganoNanos capable of tracking up to around eleven million squillion particles or about three people. Variable Time Transference Velocity, two hundred Ergo Watt WhenLock, ten thousand JumpSite Pre-sets, plus an all new Particle Oscillating Search Transfer system. Send you anywhere to a half nanosecond accuracy. P.O.S.T. it's called." Theodore stopped and deflated a little. "Well, that's what it's meant to have, anyway."

"It's broken?" asked Jules.

"I don't know. It's different. I just didn't expect this. I'm present. I'm in your present. We're all in the same Now. Not meant to happen."

"Ummm," said Jules. "I really want to ask a question here, I'm just not sure what it should be."

"How does it work?" asked Gen.

"Good question," said Theo. "I don't know."

"You don't know?"

"I don't know. Only six people know how it works, and none of them are my age."

"Got a general idea?" asked Gen.

"General idea? We slip out of the present," replied Theodore. "We stop being in the present. Once you're not in the present, you can go anywhen you like. Well, the JumpMan can send you anywhen you like. And when you get there you stay out of the present—usually just a little bit behind local time. Sometimes ahead, which is fun too, but usually behind. So we're invisible. You can't see us, because we're actually about ten nanoseconds in the past. That's not what's happening here. I'm present. I'm on local time."

"You can't just go back?" asked Jules, who hadn't understood a word of what Theodore had just said, but felt like this might have been the question he was wanting to ask before.

"I don't know. I don't know what's happening," said Theodore. "Something's gone terribly wrong. If I go back, I just don't know what will happen."

Jules and Gen thought about all this for a bit. Or rather, they tried to think about things for a bit. Gen felt a bit like her head had turned into a tumble-dryer and Jules was feeling a touch exhausted from trying to understand what Theodore was saying and keeping his brain from running off again. This time it was threatening not just to go to its office, but to go home, pack up and go on a very long holiday, and come back when Theodore had left.

Then something occurred to Jules.

"Are you sure you're not meant to be here?" he asked.

"What do you mean?" replied Theodore.

"Didn't you say this was the first one? A new JumpMan or something? Maybe you're meant to be seen and this is where you're meant to be."

Jules felt quite pleased. He was sure he'd come up with an interesting idea and a strong possibility.

"Yip, that'd be it, Dodoboy." Theodore had a way of looking at Jules as though he was some kind of excretion. Perhaps from a festering pimple. Perhaps from a rotting piece of food. But something very unwanted. He never looked at Gen that way, Jules had noticed. She could ask anything and he was very happy to answer.

"First prize in the biggest competition ever was a Jump to a brand-new JumpSite that no one has ever seen," Theodore continued. "You know last weekend, I went to Pirate Raid, Roman Battle, Three Seconds After the Big Bang, and the Opening Night of Hamlet. I don't want to be rude, but Girl's Bedroom Mil 3 is not going to be a big hit back where I come from. Secondly, what I am doing right now, standing here, you looking at me and me talking and telling you all this stuff is breaking the most fundamental rule of TimeJumping. You never break this rule. Without this rule, you cannot TimeJump; it just wouldn't be possible."

Theodore paused and looked at them.

"What's the rule?" asked Jules.

"Thought you'd never ask," said Theodore. "One Rule And One Rule Only: Don't Touch Anything."

Jules waited a moment, thinking Theodore had more to say.

When Theodore didn't say any more but stood there like he'd just delivered the Ten Commandments, Jules said, "That's it?"

"That's it," said Theodore.

"Don't Touch Anything?"

"Yip."

"But apart from that, you can do anything you like?"

"Well, if you can't touch anything, Dodoboy," said Theodore slowly, "there's not much else you can do but look, is there?" He sighed deeply like he was being forced to talk to a much lesser species.

"So you're stuck here?" Gen said.

"I'm stuck here."

"You can't fix it, or do anything with it, right?" she asked.

"No, I don't think so. There should be a Test Mode or something on it, so I can run some checks, but that'll take a while."

They all went quiet. Jules was feeling a little bruised from Theodore's patronizing of him, Gen was feeling a bit worried about his continued presence, and Theodore was turning the JumpMan over and over, trying to find something.

"So what are you going to do?" asked Gen.

"Wait," replied Theodore. "I was only meant to be gone five minutes, so someone must be looking for me by now." He shrugged. "They'll turn up, and like I said, there'll be some Code Cops here, they'll do a Rewind, get time back into balance, and it'll be like this never happened."

Gen had a worried look on her face.

"Wait? Do you mean here? You want to wait here?"

"Can't I?" asked Theodore.

"How long do you want to wait for?"

"I don't know. Maybe five minutes. Maybe a couple of days."

Gen looked alarmed.

"You can't hang around here for a couple of days!"

"Why not? I'm very charming. I'll let you wear my Coat."

"No, I mean, you'll get caught. *We'll* get caught. Mum already thinks she's seen you. She actually finds you and she'll kick me out of here. I'm not sharing with Cynthia again."

"Oh, no, I won't get caught. It's bad enough you two know. No one else can find out. That could be serious. You have to hide me."

"How am I going to hide you? What do you mean?" Gen was getting increasingly frustrated with the situation.

"Well, it's the TimeCode," said Theodore, getting off Gen's bed and pacing about. "I mean, I've already changed history. This is not meant to happen or it would have already happened. You two are not meant to know about the future. You're not meant to even know that there is a future. You see what I mean about the rule? Talking to you, you seeing me, it's touching stuff. It's touching you, and it changes history. History now includes you two who are the only people in Mil 3 who know about the future. That there is a future and that TimeJumping is possible. That's a lot to know. No one else can find out."

Theodore sat down. He'd become very serious during that lengthy speech and he was looking at them now like it was crunch time. They had to decide what they were going to do.

Gen breathed out heavily, shook her head, and said, "I don't believe you."

"What?" said Theodore.

"It's not possible," she argued. "Time travel. It's not possible."

"TimeJumping."

"Jumping, hopping, skipping, whatever! It's just not possible."

"Well, how do you think I got here?" asked Theodore.

"I don't know, but why haven't we seen any of you before? Why doesn't history change all the time, if you lot are always jumping about it? If I could jump about history, I'd want to change it. Look at all the dumb stuff that's happened. Maybe you should go and change things. And what if you went back and looked at yourself? Couldn't you tell yourself the answers to an exam or the winning numbers in Lotto, and wouldn't everyone want to do that?"

Again, Jules was amazed at Gen's ability to keep up with all this. He was still being distracted by Theodore's hair, which was now a broad stripe of yellow with red and green lightning bolts flashing on either side, and whenever the time travel stuff came up he could feel the entire concept slipping away from him, like most of what his math teacher said.

"We can't do any of that," said Theodore. "We have a very strict rule."

"What, 'Don't Touch Anything'? That's the kind of rule we have for Cynthia when we go to my grandmother's. That's not a rule for hopping around everywhere."

"Everywhen, actually," corrected Theodore.

"Oh shut up. Why are you correcting me? You can't even say OK. It's just the two letters. O and K. OK?"

"Is it? Is it really?" Theodore looked amazed. "Is that what it is? In my time we say 'oak eye,' and everyone thought it meant like the eye of an oak. It isn't a very old and sacred expression? You mean, it's just the two letters, O and K? That's so funny. Why?"

"I don't know why. Stop asking me why to all the stuff that's just stuff, will you?"

Gen stomped around for a moment and then stood in front of Theodore, a furious look on her face.

"You went somewhere before, didn't you?" she asked.

"Oh, that," said Theodore. "That was a JumpOut. That still seems to be working. It's an emergency thing. You arrive in the middle of a lava flow or the middle of a big war or something, it jumps you a hundred years into the future and hopefully things might have calmed down a little."

"Is that where you went? Here, but in a hundred years?" asked Jules, forgetting that he was the stupid one and getting caught up in Theodore's talk. He was still torn between wanting Theodore to go and wanting him to stay. In general, he believed Theodore. He just didn't understand him.

"Yes," answered Theodore. "And believe me, in a hundred years time this place is not pretty."

"Well, take me somewhere that is pretty," demanded Gen.

"*Take* you somewhere?" Theodore looked astonished. "I can't take you anywhere. This thing is not working all that well. I'm stuck here, remember, because it's not working properly. We could go somewhere and never come back."

"You're just making all this up."

"Oh, and why would I bother? Believe me, if I could be out of here I would. Being stuck here is worse than going to the Moon for a tour of the Tranquillity Industrial Park."

"You go to the Moon?" asked Jules.

"You've never been to the Moon?" asked Theodore. "Forget about it, it's not a patch on Mars."

"You go to Mars?"

"Oh shut up, Jules!" screamed Gen in a tired and frustrated voice. "You're only egging him on. He's making it up.

There's something weird going on, but it's not all this. There has to be a far simpler explanation for what this annoying headache-causing idiot is doing in my room!"

Theodore looked at her and raised an eyebrow.

"Hang on then, just let me check something."

He picked up the remote, pointed it at the JumpMan, and disappeared.

A few seconds later he came back.

"Yip, that seems fine. Come on, then." He grabbed Gen by the hand, turned to her, and said, "Close your eyes," and then he pressed the Go button on the remote.

They both disappeared.

Jules was alone.

~ Where did they go? his brain asked.

~ Oh, how would I know? replied Jules, and even the voice inside his head sounded tiny and scared.

~ Do you think he's telling the truth?

~ I hope he is, said Jules. Because if he isn't, then I'm really going to start to freak out.

Meanwhile . . .

QUINCY CARTER ONE LAY ON THE LONG GREY COUCH IN HIS OFFICE. His eyes were closed and he was massaging his temples. He was not a man who panicked. He was not a man who worried. He never usually had to. He was Cheeo of the biggest company on the two planets. He hadn't built that company up by leaving things to chance or making mistakes.

So how could things have gone so completely and disastrously wrong tonight? Where was the kid? Why hadn't he come back? Five minutes he was meant to be gone. It was now getting on for three hours. The launch of the new JumpMan Pro had been screened everywhere. The finale was meant to be a live link to the amazing new JumpSite that Theodore Pine was meant to be at.

He didn't get there.

Quincy felt sick at the memory of that long hour he'd stayed on stage. Stalling, spinning out stories, anything in the hope that the kid would either turn up where he was meant to be or simply come back.

No sign of him. At least that dizzy-headed fool of a Vice Cheeo for Publicity, Honeydew Meloni, had managed to stop the networks from screening pictures of the JumpSite where Theo wasn't.

And at least Quincy had managed to sound convincing when he announced that there'd been some slight technical difficulties and, well, thanks for coming but that was the end of the show.

He'd rushed back to his office, slammed the door shut, and was refusing any calls. There'd be time for all of that soon. Right now he needed some space to think.

There was a knock at the door.

The sound caught him by surprise. No one ever knocked on his door. They spoke over intercoms or they arrived by appointment, they never just knocked.

He swung off the couch, walked over, and opened the door.

"Quin—umm, I mean, Mr. Carter?" Honeydew was visibly shaking.

"This better be important, Meloni. I'd hate to think of you doing publicity for the Dust Sifters on the dark side of the Moon for the rest of your career."

Again, Honeydew was shocked at the dead-eyed, hateful gaze being levelled at her by the usually jolly old Quincy.

"Well, Mr. and Mrs. Pine are here."

It took Quincy a moment and then he straightened up and looked out past her into the reception area.

"His parents," continued Honeydew. "They want to know what happened."

"Not half as much as I do, Meloni. He's only their kid. I've got much more at stake."

Honeydew was getting scared. Whatever was going on, it had changed her lovable boss into someone she didn't even recognize.

"Show 'em in. And Meloni?"

"Yes?" she answered timidly.

"At this point, you'll be lucky if you end up on the dark side of the Moon."

Honeydew backed away, her eyes wide with fear, and headed for the reception area to get Theodore's parents.

chapter three

No Time Like the Present

Sand, thought Gen. Lots of sand. Either there's suddenly a lot of sand in my bedroom or I'm somewhere else.

She could feel hot sunshine. Extremely hot sunshine. It was making the sand hot and she lifted up her legs to stop her feet burning. Her eyes struggled to adjust to the sudden brightness that blasted at her from above and bounced up at her off the yellow-white sand. There seemed to be no shade anywhere and as far as she could tell she was sitting on a high point somewhere in the middle of a vast expanse of sand.

"Theodore," she asked quietly, "this is not a beach, is it?"

"Mmmm? Don't make too much noise," he whispered. "No one is really going to pay any attention to us, but we are visible. I wasn't sure what would happen to you, but you're present just like me. This is so unboid. Anyway, right now your boyfriend is probably feeling a bit lonely."

"He's not my boyfriend!"

"Uh-huh. He wants to be."

Gen would have liked to continue the discussion but she was starting to catch up with the fact that she was definitely no longer in her bedroom.

The amount of sunshine starting to fry her was one clue. The other clues were the dust, noise, and stink coming from the valley that stretched out for several miles below the low sand dune on which they were sitting.

The air was thick with dust. Tiny dry grains burnt her nostrils and her throat every time she breathed in. She held one hand over her mouth and attempted to shade her eyes from the glare with the other. Below her, great clouds of dust were being raised by some kind of activity that she still couldn't make out.

The noise was incredible. There was a great grinding

going on, sounding somewhere between the fingernails of a huge hand being scraped along an immense blackboard and a very slow avalanche. There were occasional long, drawn-out shrieks as though some rocks were being born and then what felt like great subterranean rumbles and thumps. Accompanying this was the sound of chanting, as though a choir of ten thousand voices was performing at the end of the world.

The stink was unbelievable. It was bad enough trying not to breathe in the hot air thick with grit but the air stank with a sour smell that it took Gen a while to place. It was stale sweat. Great wafts of it coming from the dust bowl in the valley below her.

Gen was overwhelmed by her own senses. She wanted to close them all down. She leaned over to Theodore.

"OK, I believe you. Can we go now?" Gen was starting to feel very scared.

"Oh, come on. Aren't you even going to look?"

She half opened her eyes. She could see a little better now and in the clouds of dust she could make out what seemed to be thousands of men, stripped to the waist, straining to pull and push huge blocks of stone across the valley floor. Thick ropes were attached to the blocks and lines of men hundreds of yards long were hauling on them. They were heading toward a great stone platform about a mile away. Around the platform were ramps, and more teams of men were hauling giant slabs of the sandy-colored rock up the ramps and into position on the platform.

Scurrying around the teams of men were women and children, carrying water. The water was being poured on the ground, sprayed onto the bodies of the teams of men hauling the stones, and poured down their throats.

Gen looked at the platform. There was something familiar about it. Or half familiar at least. She couldn't quite figure out what they were building, what all this effort was for. It didn't seem like they were building a big hall or a big house. It looked solid, with a broad square base a few hundred yards long on each side and smoothly rising walls on a steep angle up to the level where men were dragging stones.

If they keep going like that, she thought, it'll be pointy on the top. Like a pyramid.

That was when Gen knew she really wasn't in her bedroom.

Instead, she was watching the building of the Great Pyramid at Khufu. In front of her was rising the most famous structure ever built. Back in her time, people still debated how the pyramids were constructed. When she got back, she could say, "Well, when I was last there, they used a lot of men to drag the stones over wet clay and up ramps."

Theodore was watching Gen watching the building of the Great Pyramid at Khufu. He was smirking and when she turned to look at him, he burst out laughing.

"That's fantastic. I've Jumped with some first-timers before, but I never Jumped with anyone who didn't even know you could Jump. That was just great. Do you know where you are?"

"Yes, I think. Is that what I think it is?"

"Well, if you think it's the Great Wall of China, nip it's not," said Theodore. "Yip, it's the Great Pyramid. You know the pyramids are still there, in Fifteen Billion and Seventy-three? They were one of the first things we found. So when TimeJumping was invented, this was one of the first Jumps anyone did. Pretty amazing, eh?"

Gen felt like she was dreaming. Or more that she was in a dream and dreaming that she was dreaming. But she was also almost vibrating from head to toe with excitement and sheer aliveness. This was a sensation beyond sensation. She'd ridden on the fastest rides, she'd seen some great films, she'd kissed a boy, but this . . . this was . . .

"Amazing," she whispered, now completely dazed by it all.

Theodore stood up. "Want to take a closer look?"

"What do you mean?"

"Let's go down, have a look around. Look how many

people are down there. No one's going to notice us." Theodore's hair went to jet black.

"Here, have The Coat." With a gallant gesture, Theodore took off The Coat and flung it around Gen's shoulders. "Desert robes, Coat. Building of Pyramids style."

The Coat changed into light flowing robes with a hood, which Gen pulled up over her head. Theo's shirt took on the same dusty color and his pants looked like he'd been hauling rocks through the desert for years. He kicked off his shoes and stuck them in a pocket.

"Come on," he said.

They joined a shuffling line of women and children hauling water.

"This is fantastic," whispered Theo. "We're joining in!"

"Isn't it illegal or something? What about the Rule?"

"The TimeCode? Woosh, what harm can this do? We're still just having a look."

The line shuffled on. The women were all dark-haired and hooded, the children bright-eyed and strong. They didn't seem overjoyed to be lugging camel-skin bags full of water but they didn't seem that unhappy about it.

"Where're the whips?" asked Gen.

"Whips?"

"You know, I thought there'd be big guys in leather

masks whipping the slaves on. Slobbering dogs or something. Everyone's just doing it."

"Oh, there's not that many slaves doing this. These are farmers and brickmakers and their wives and kids. They're rostered on pyramid duty while the Nile's in flood. Nothing else to do. If they do this, they don't have to pay as much tax."

Building the pyramids was a tax dodge? thought Gen. She was an accountant's daughter after all. Dad'd love this, she thought.

The line had reached the toiling men. There seemed to be a thousand of them hauling in rhythm. The women slopped water onto the ground and with each surging effort the stone moved forward. Only a little, but there were ten groups of a thousand men, all hauling at the one large rock. Move the rock a little each day and before you know it, a couple of decades have gone by, and the Pharaoh's got himself a pretty nice pyramid to lie in for eternity.

Theodore stopped to look at the structure. Even though it was only half built, it was inspiring. The pyramid seemed to be rising perfectly and effortlessly from the plain. It looked as though it should be there.

As well as a tax dodge, perhaps being part of the most happening civilization yet gave everybody a bit of a buzz, thought Gen.

Theodore pulled out the JumpMan and it hovered in front of him. Some of the women nearby looked at them in alarm and started to chatter and point in their direction.

"What are you doing?" asked Gen.

Theodore shrugged. "Well, that'll do, won't it? You believe me now? Better get going."

"Hey! You two. Stop!" A man had let go of his rope and was now rushing over to them.

"Stop!"

Theodore grabbed Gen by the hand and with the other started to fumble with the remote.

"Wait! Are you looking for me? I'm Franklin Nixon. Franklin Nixon One. You looking for me?"

Theodore stopped fumbling with the remote.

"Franklin Nixon? *The* Franklin Nixon?"

The Franklin Nixon puffing from running managed a nod.

"Unfortunately, yes," he replied after getting his breath. "Quick, put that thing away. It's a Jumper, right? You must be my search party. Come over here, quick. People are starting to notice and they don't like anything here that's out of order."

The Franklin Nixon shepherded them over to a water bag, dipped a cup into the bag, and drank deeply. He made Gen grab the JumpMan and hide it in her robes. Gen felt alarmed to have the machine in her hands but was even more terrified of this strange skinny old man who'd run out of the rock-hauling line and seemed to know all about them.

"Took your time, didn't you?"

The skinny old man had a long, sad, exhausted face, but his eyes were bright and eager. There was almost a greedy look in them, Gen thought.

"Um, Franklin," said Theodore. "I'm sorry, but we're not your search party."

"What? Whaddya mean? What are you doing here, then? Why are you visible?"

"Well, that's a long story, but you've been gone for years. I don't think anyone's looking for you."

The old man's face got even sadder, and the bright look went out of his eyes.

"I mean, we know all about you," Theodore hurried to add. "You're a hero. There's a museum and everything."

"I got a museum?"

"Yeah, there's your original device, and an empty bed and a plaque and all your work. It's your lab just as you left it."

"I got a plaque? What's it say?"

Gen noticed that people were moving away from them. They were attracting attention. She wondered if she should point this out, but Franklin and Theodore seemed to have a lot to catch up on.

"Pheeps, um, it's been a while since I went there," said Theodore. "We all go there when we're about seven, but I think it says something like: 'On This Spot, Franklin Nixon One Attempted the First Manned TimeJump. His last words were, "Here goes nothing."'"

Franklin laughed a sad laugh.

"They were too! How wrong can a guy be?"

"True," said Theodore. "But we still remember you. You're even in the language."

"What do you mean?" asked Franklin suspiciously.

"Ah, well, we say 'Lucky as Franklin,' or 'You've got Franklin's chance of that happening,' or 'I've had a real Franklin of a day' . . ."

"Yeah, well, thanks kid. But that's not how I was hoping to be remembered."

Franklin fell silent and looked at the scene around him with great weariness. "I was here when the astronomers laid out the foundations. I don't want to be here when they finish the thing."

Gen coughed nervously. People near them were muttering and pointing. Everyone else was busy and organized into a specific purpose. No one else was standing around chatting.

"Um, I'm sorry," she said, "but everyone's pointing at us. Theodore, shouldn't we get going?"

Theodore turned to her shaking his head.

"Gen! Don't you realize who this is? We've just solved one of TimeJumping's oldest mysteries. What happened to Franklin Nixon? Where did he go? He wasn't meant to Jump until the next day, but when they came to his lab, he'd gone."

"Hmmph." Franklin grunted. "I just thought I should test it. I slipped out of the present, particle scan was fine, set the dial about twelve nanoseconds out of synch, bang I'm here. It was fantastic. I got right into the Pharaoh's palace. He was having a dinner party. No problem. I'm taking a look around, it was fantastic. All of a sudden, just as the feature dish comes out—Roasted Rhino served on a Corn Polenta with a Scarab Beetle Jus—I'm present. I felt this tiny little jolt, and snap, everyone's looking at me. I had my finger in the sauce. I just wanted a little taste. Try explaining that to a Pharaoh who feeds his crocodiles with people who sneeze while he's speaking. I don't know what went wrong."

"Umm, it was your wife, Franklin," said Theodore.

"What?"

"She didn't know you'd Jumped. She came in to use the computer to z-mail her sister. She pressed Send and it must have somehow sent you into the present. You hadn't saved yourself, and no one knew where you'd gone."

"Everyone knew where!" Franklin yelled. "Chester, George, all of them knew this was going to be the first Jump. Quincy did the original calculations. He knew. It was such a great question to answer. How did the pyramids get here? Who built these things? Great publicity for the Time Travel Six. Why hasn't anyone come looking for me?"

Gen was getting frightened. Franklin had started to yell and look very angry.

"I've been here for forty years! No one's come here since?"

Theodore looked uncomfortable again.

"Sorry, Franklin, thousands of people have been here. It's a really popular Site. Standard pre-set on all JumpMans. It's a training Jump. It's one of the first we do."

Franklin looked astonished and slumped down on the sand.

"Oh, I don't believe this. I've been here under everyone's nose, for forty years, and no one noticed?"

"Well, no one told us to look. And we're all invisible, and we're way over there."

Theodore pointed at the dune where he and Gen had just come from.

"Where? There're people there now?" Franklin struggled to his feet. "Hey, it's me. Franklin Nixon. Come and get me!" He waved and yelled like a madman in the direction Theo had pointed.

"Shhh!" hissed Gen. "Whips!" A giant of a man was looking over at them. He had bulging muscles, metal rings on his arms, and a whip made of plaited leather and metal studs.

"Oak eye, oak eye," said Franklin, quieting down a little. "Everyone's invisible, you say? So that's what they went with? No one Jumps visible?"

"No, it's against the Code. Don't Touch Anything."

Franklin groaned.

"Oh, that's awful. Is that the best they could do? In my day, it was 'Leave Well Enough Alone' and we had a huge fight getting someone to work on changing that."

He sighed and slumped to the sand again. Things seemed to have settled down. The work had stopped for the moment and the people seemed to be in the middle of a shift change. Everyone was moving about and so no one was really taking any notice of them. Gen tried to lift Franklin's mood.

"It must have been great to be here," she said. "You know everything, you're from the future, you could do anything you like."

Franklin looked at her like she was a silly little girl.

"Yeah well, once they decided I wasn't a god, I spent

a long time in the Pharaoh's service. I wasn't fed to the crocodiles. I had to feed the crocodiles. It's not a job where you draw attention to yourself. I learnt the language. I just tried to fit in. Show me the Jumper!"

Gen looked at Theodore who nodded slowly, but the look on his face seemed to be warning her of something. "Stay close to me," he mouthed. Gen handed Theodore the JumpMan and he held it up for Franklin to see, while with his other hand, he worked the remote behind his back.

"TimeMaster JumpMan Pro," said Theodore. "Latest model."

"Woosh, look at the thing," said Franklin. "Mine took up all of the spare room and most of the front verandah."

"I know," said Theo. "I've seen it at the museum."

"Bet everyone thinks it's hilarious," said Franklin. "Mind if I take a look at it? I'd love to see inside." He held up a couple of wooden wedges and a mallet.

"Maybe not," said Theodore, backing away and keeping Gen behind him. He muttered "Get ready" out of the corner of his mouth.

"I don't want to get sand in it," he continued. "It's brand-new."

"Hummph. Did you say TimeMaster?"

"Yeah, TimeMaster Corporation. That's who makes them."

"That was my name for the company," said Franklin.

"Really? Quincy Carter always claims he came up with it," said Theodore, immediately wishing he hadn't.

"Lying toad. They're all rich, right? The Time Travel Six. Or Five, I suppose without me."

"Rich? They seem all right," said Theodore, starting to realize what would set Franklin off.

"And here I am!" Franklin shouted. "Three months a year on pyramid duty, then I have to go and help plant wheat after the Nile subsides, then the crop gets eaten by locusts and we all starve and die of plague and those stinking five . . . Give me the Jumper!"

Gen leapt back. A sudden change had come over Franklin Nixon One. He was no longer the gloomy, morose figure he'd been. Now he was wiry and angry. His eyes were wide, his lips sneering, and his nostrils flared. He leapt at Theodore, who slipped and then ducked away into the crowd.

"Give it to me! It's mine. I invented it! I'm Jumping out of here and don't anyone try to stop me!"

"Gen," yelled Theodore. "Keep up with me!"

Theodore was dodging about and Gen kept losing sight of him. He wasn't much of a runner, but he managed to duck into the line of hauling men, directly in front of a giant piece of rock. Gen followed, slipped, and looked up to see the line of men about to stamp straight on over her and haul the rock on top of her. These lines didn't stop for anything once they'd started.

Franklin appeared just on the other side of the line and flung himself at her. She screamed as he disappeared in mid-fling.

Theodore wove back through the lines of men, grabbed her, and dragged her out.

"Where's he gone? What happened?" yelled Theodore.

"I don't know," screamed Gen, now completely freaked out. The background noise of rumbling rocks and men chanting was thumping in her ears. "Can we go now?" she begged.

"Grab my hand," Theodore shouted.

Gen did so and closed her eyes as Theodore pressed the Go button on the remote.

Jules had gone weak at the knees, light in the head, dry in the mouth, sweaty in the palms, cold up his spine, and sick in the pit of his stomach when Gen and Theodore had disappeared. Like Gen, he'd been listening to Theodore, and even though he believed him, his brain kept insisting, whenever it wasn't off hiding somewhere, that time travel just wasn't possible. And even if it was, how could it be something that kids did on the weekend? So when Theodore had grabbed Gen by the hand and just *phoooop*—gone, Jules had to sit down and try to take it all in.

~ *OK, said his brain, I'm taking it in.*

~ *Thank you, said Jules. You're not going to hide?*

~ *It's not hiding. That's instinct. I have to protect myself.*

~ *Sure, sure.*

Jules paced up and down the room.

Then he paced from side to side.

He tried the diagonal, and then around and around in a small circle.

They'd been gone a long time. And they still weren't back.

He sat back on Gen's bed and picked up a magazine.

It was on the top of a pile on her bedside table. All of them had pop stars and pouting models on the front and he'd opened at random to a page that contained a quiz: "Are You Ready For A Boyfriend? Take Our Special Quiz and You'll Find Out." Question three caught his attention.

When He Asks You Out, Do You:

(a) Faint.

(b) Turn into a dribbling idiot.

(c) Have trouble remembering your own name.

(d) Give him a long cool stare and say, "I'm not sure.

I may be going skiing with Raoul this weekend."

Gen hadn't done any of that with him. It was more like she'd:

(a) Completely ignored him.

(b) Didn't even register that he'd asked.

(c) Felt slightly queasy at the thought of him asking.

(d) Immediately got a better offer from an older kid with astonishing hair and some pretty neat gear.

Jules couldn't decide if that meant she was ready or not. Maybe she just wasn't ready for him.

He sat there flicking through the magazine over and over again.

~ *Kid, you going to read that? Because I'm getting really sick of you trying to ignore it.*

~ *Sorry, brain, replied Jules. I was just trying to distract myself.*

~ *Yeah, well I don't have that option. I'm your brain, and even though you haven't noticed it, I've seen that ad for G-Lux glitter eye shadow nine times now, and I don't want to see it again.*

~ *Sorry, sorry, I'm sorry.*

Jules threw the magazine on the floor.

"But where are they?" he asked out loud.

"Where's who?" asked Katherine opening the door and coming into the room.

Jules swung around to face her and started thinking desperately.

"Where are they, where . . . are . . . they . . . thinking . . . of . . . going . . . tomorrow?" He nodded, trying to look like that's what he'd really meant to say all along.

"What are you talking about? Who's they? Where's Genevieve?"

"Genevieve? She's, ahh, in the bathroom."

Katherine's eyebrows twitched around violently like electrocuted caterpillars.

"I was just in the bathroom. She's not in the bathroom. It's happening again, isn't it? There's something going on! You kids are up to something!"

Katherine ran back to the door and yelled down the stairs.

"Steven! Tony! Get up here. Now. Genevieve's gone!"

At the precise moment she leaned out the door to yell at her husband and Jules's dad, Theodore and Gen reappeared. Jules leapt in the air.

"Hide!" he hissed at Theodore, and Theodore did another JumpOut.

Gen hurriedly brushed sand off her clothes and tried to look like she'd been there all the time. Katherine turned back into the room, and screamed.

"Aaaahhhhhh! Where did you . . . ? What . . . ? How did

you . . . ? You couldn't have . . ." Katherine couldn't finish sentences again.

"What is it, Mum?" Gen tried to look more like someone who'd just been rearranging her bookshelf or smoothing her doona, rather than someone who'd just gotten back from their first TimeJump to four and a half thousand years ago.

Jules tried to look equally innocent, and they both looked as guilty as shoplifters with bulging coats.

Tony and Steven came in with Cynthia peering excitedly around their legs. Her mother had screamed! Gotta be something good going on.

"What? What is it?" Steven asked looking concerned.

"Genevieve. She disappeared. She's back. There's someone else. She knows. He knows. Look at them. Ask them!"

Steven looked from one to the other. "Gen," he said. "Did you just disappear?"

"No, Dad." Gen had a sweet I'm-so-sorry-but-I-know-you-had-to-ask-me-look and Jules did a very good confused shake of the head. Well, at least it felt all right until he caught Cynthia's eye. She was staring straight at him and he immediately felt trapped.

"I think it's time we were going, Jules," suggested Tony. "Come on."

Jules tried to think of an excuse to stay but Gen gave him a small shake of the head and a wave and he gathered that he'd better go. He went downstairs with his dad, with Katherine muttering behind them, Steven scratching his head, and Cynthia sniggering. At the front door, they said quick good-byes and then he and his dad were walking up the street back to their place.

"You want to tell me what all that was about?" asked his dad, once they were out of earshot of the Corrigans.

Not really, thought Jules.

"Dunno, Dad," he said. "Mrs. Corrigan just went weird on us."

"Did she what!" said Tony. After a little pause, he said, "You know that's the first time I've seen them since, ah, well, since you and your mother left."

Jules looked up at his dad. He'd been back with his dad for a month now, and that was the first time he'd said anything about Jules going away, or his mother leaving, or anything like that.

"Really? Aren't you friends and stuff?" he asked.

"Yeah, well, I'd see Steven a bit, have lunch and things like that. But going over there, like we used to, it just never happened."

They lapsed into silence, both thinking about Angela, Jules's mum.

"She all right? Your mum, I mean." Tony tried to sound casual.

Oh, this is getting heavy, thought Jules. I wish I'd just told him about Theodore.

"Yeah. She's fine," said Jules neutrally.

They walked through their own gate. Tony opened the front door and they both went inside.

"Better get up to bed, mate. It's late. I'll see you in the morning."

They both stood a little awkwardly for a moment or two. Should they hug? Was he too old to kiss his dad? Tony settled it by reaching out and giving Jules's bicep a squeeze. Jules smiled and turned and went upstairs.

He thought he'd be too excited to sleep. Where had Theodore and Gen gone? Where was Theodore now?

~ Can we think about this in the morning, please? asked his brain.

Good idea, thought Jules and fell asleep, exhausted, about three seconds later.

Meanwhile . . .

IT WAS A CHARMING, COMPLETELY CONCERNED, WORRIED ONLY FOR THEIR CHILD QUINCY CARTER ONE WHO HAD JUST PARTED COMPANY WITH MR. AND MRS. PINE. As of now, he'd declared, TimeMaster Corporation was concerned with only one thing: finding Theodore and getting him home.

"Everything possible," he'd assured them. "And we'll probably try some things that aren't," he quipped but while smiling in such a compassionate way that they never felt for an instant that he was making light of their distress.

After they'd gone to consult with the TimeJumping search parties that were now heading out to all known JumpSites, Quincy had headed back through his office. He had a nagging feeling that somewhere back in here was the answer to what had gone wrong. Doors programmed to open only for him, slid open and he walked through into his workshop.

He picked up a TimeScanner, let his gaze roam around the workshop for a moment, and then turned to walk out again. And then he stopped. He'd seen something that wasn't quite right. He turned around and looked again. His mind slowly filled with horror. His stomach started to churn as he, Quincy Carter One, the smartest and richest man on two planets, realized he'd done something really dumb.

He walked over to his titanium-topped workbench. Sitting on it was a JumpMan. Beside it the usual red remote.

Quincy shook his head slowly and felt a real pain in his temples.

This was not the JumpMan that should be sitting there.

Back here, in his very private, very secret workshop, should be a very private, very secret JumpMan. A prototype of a new kind of JumpMan that would revolutionize TimeJumping and make him, Quincy Carter One, so impossibly rich, that as he'd been developing this radical new machine, he would sometimes be overwhelmed by the potential wealth it was going to generate.

But that prototype, secret JumpMan was not sitting on his workbench. Instead, here was the TimeMaster JumpMan Pro. The JumpMan Theodore should have.

Quincy turned and ran out of his workshop.

He couldn't have! He couldn't have made such a string of simple mistakes. He couldn't have picked up the wrong JumpMan, then forgot about it, then sent Honeydew back to pick it up, and then . . . and then . . . and then . . .

He gazed wildly around his office. He remembered putting the JumpMan in his bottom drawer—that's right, he did realize it was the wrong one, so he'd put it in the bottom drawer . . . He flung it open. There was no JumpMan.

If his office and workshop weren't so lush, isolated, and soundproof, then possibly people for many miles around would have heard a cry of anguish and pain so horrendous and filled with such desperate frustration that they would have remembered it for the rest of their days. He, Quincy Carter One, one of the six people on the two planets who knew exactly how TimeJumping worked, and really the only one actually still functioning, was about to lose everything because a fourteen-year-old boy was somewhere in the last fifteen billion years with the key to his future.

Although, he thought, as he slumped back onto the long grey couch and tried to calm himself, if he's got the prototype of the Next Generation JumpMan, I have a fair idea where young Theodore Pine might be.

chapter four

Making Up for Lost Time

Is that the time already? The clock told Jules he'd been asleep for seven hours. How come it felt like ten minutes? While he'd been asleep he'd been convinced that he wasn't asleep at all. But as he groaned and stretched and felt his body returning to him, Jules realized he'd actually been quite deeply asleep all night. He gave up trying to figure it out and lay there letting the alarm ring out.

~ Good move, said his brain.

~ What is? Jules asked.

~ Lying around here, doing nothing, stretching, feeling cozy while he's over at Gen's place.

Jules sat bolt upright in bed.

Theodore!

Gen!

Had all that actually happened? Last night? Theodore turning up with that hair and The Coat? Then he and Gen disappearing? All of last night's questions raced back into his head. He started buzzing around his room. Got to get going. Got to get to Gen's, before she goes to school. Got to get to school . . .

~ Yes, OK, said his brain. Could you go and have a shower so I can wake up, please?

After his shower, Jules ran downstairs into the kitchen.

"Morning," said his dad, putting bread into the toaster.

"Dad," said Jules.

"Can I get something straight here?" asked his dad.

Oh no, thought Jules. He's been thinking about last night. He's figured something out. What does he want?

His dad fixed him with a puzzled look. "Do you go through an entire box of cereal in about two days?"

Phew!

"Umm, yeah, pretty much," said Jules.

"When?"

"When what?"

"When? When do you eat it all?"

Jules added it up. Two full bowls in the morning, two or three when he got home. Another one if he was up late and needed a snack before bed. He told his father.

"I should buy the big boxes then," said his dad.

"Yeah," said Jules. "You know, or get something else."

"What do you mean?"

"Well, there's nothing else to eat here, Dad. You know, you need some packets of corn chips and some dips, and a few frozen pizzas, and packets of biscuits and crackers, and cheese and stuff like that. Then I don't have to just eat cereal."

Tony nodded, fascinated by the diet of his thirteen-year-old boy.

"Fruit?" he suggested.

"Yeah, well, if you can't get the other stuff."

Tony laughed.

"I'll get some fruit as well."

Jules nodded and went upstairs to get his things for school. He came back into the kitchen.

"I better get going, Dad. I need to get my homework done."

Tony looked up.

"I thought you and Gen were up there doing it last night?"

Whoops. They'd been getting on so well, Jules had told the truth. Time for the lie.

"Oh, no, that's an assignment we're doing together. I didn't get much of my other homework done."

Tony gave him a strange look that went for a bit too long, but then just nodded and returned to the newspaper.

"Yeah, OK. See you tonight."

"See you, Dad." Jules scurried out of the house, feeling like he'd just had a narrow escape.

Should he head to Gen's place? He didn't normally turn up there at eight o'clock in the morning. And if he did today, would it be friendly Gen or snooty Gen who would greet him?

~ *So many questions.*

~ *Ah, brain. If you had as many answers, I wouldn't have so many questions.*

~ *Oh, I've got the answers. You just have to decide which question.*

~ *I have to find out what happened last night.*

~ *I was hoping you'd think that.*

~ *Let's go.*

As Jules approached Gen's house, he saw Theodore sitting on a neighbor's fence. His hair was a kind of relaxed violet, his clothes were a reasonable facsimile of what

Jules himself was wearing, and he was gazing around at everything in the street.

He didn't notice Jules, and as Jules got closer he could see Theodore banging his heels into the fence and could hear him talking to himself.

"No one knows I'm here," he was saying. "No one came looking for Franklin. No one knows I'm here. This is not good."

"Hi," said Jules. "You're still here! What's not good?"

Theodore turned around, a bit startled.

"What?" he said. "Oh, well yip. Or yair, as you say. I'm still here. That's not good."

"Oh," said Jules, feeling a bit awkward. "I'm glad you're here."

"Really?" said Theodore, and the two of them looked at each other a bit embarrassed and not sure what to say next. Theodore broke the moment by jumping off the fence and starting to interrogate Jules.

"Is this a dangerous time?" he asked. "Is there a war going on? Lot of dangerous animals about?"

"A war? Not around here. There's a few dogs. Some cats. I think the Hobsons have a rabbit," said Jules, feeling confused almost immediately by Theodore.

"Where did you go last night?" Jules asked.

"Last night? Oh, right. Gen and I went to the Building of

the Great Pyramid JumpSite and then when we got back, I saw her mother there again, and so I did a JumpOut, stayed a hundred years in the future for a while and then came back again."

"So the JumpMan's working?"

"Not really," answered Theodore. "I can do some stuff, but I can't go back home yet. So, you're sure there's no danger about?"

Jules looked around the street. It was the street he'd grown up in, McKernan Place, and it looked much the same as ever. Houses, footpaths, road, powerlines. What was Theodore going on about?

"I mean, your houses are so solid," he was saying. "The windows are all closed up, the blinds are down. The doors never open, and half the places have those big fences. People hardly ever come out and when they do, they just get into one of those transporter things, strap themselves in, and head off. You sure there's no danger?" Theodore actually seemed a bit nervous.

Jules looked around his street again. Suddenly it took on a very different aspect. As he watched, the front door of the place over the road from Gen's opened. A man came out and walked quickly to his car. He unlocked it, got in, put on his seatbelt, reversed quickly out of his driveway, and drove off. I suppose it could look a bit like we're kind of worried about something, he thought.

"This strip here. This is for kids only?" Theodore was pointing at the footpath.

"No," answered Jules. "Anyone can walk on it."

"Ah. This is for walking. I'd only seen two kids come by. All the adults had got into the transporters and headed off on the black stuff." Theodore gestured at the road.

"All the houses are connected by these wires." Theodore was looking up at the powerlines. "Is that how you communicate with one another?"

Amazing, thought Jules. Last night Theodore had seemed so smart. Now he didn't seem to understand the first thing about a normal suburban street.

"Well, there's telephone lines up there, but most of it's power I think. Electricity."

"You make the electricity somewhere else? And then send it around?" Theodore looked startled.

"Yeah. Why, what do you do?"

"The roof. Our roofs are all solar panels. All the power we need. Not that I should have told you that."

Jules was seeing the street through Theodore's eyes. It was all starting to look a bit strange. Why was there a strip of concrete for the footpath and then a bit of grass between that and the road? Why did some houses have trees and others a fine collection of garden ornaments?

What did people ever do with their front yard, except work in it on Sundays?

"There's another one! What's that, what did they do wrong?"

Jules was startled out of his own thoughts. Theodore was pointing up at the traffic that was going by at the next corner.

"What? I missed it, what was it?" he asked.

"Someone on a thing with just two wheels. They have to push and push and push to get it going and they're forced to ride the thing out there with all the other transporters. It's a form of punishment, right?" asked Theodore.

Jules started laughing. He wondered if he'd ever be able to look at his street and the traffic in the same way again.

"No, that's just someone on a bike, Theodore," he said. "A bicycle. They're not being punished. They want to do it."

"Really?" Theodore looked like he didn't believe him. "Mil 3 is really weird," he said to himself. "You know the only good thing is the food. And it's terrible."

"What do you mean?" Jules was laughing at him again. Theodore found everything fascinating and he had something to say about everything. He was amazing to be around.

"Gen smuggled me up some Frosted Flakes? Is that what they're called? The Coat did a quick analysis and said

I should stop eating them immediately. The Coat said there was more nutrition in dandruff. But they tasted so good! How do you people stay alive?"

The smile died a little on Jules's face and some of the joy he was feeling in Theodore's company faded away. Theodore had spent the night in Gen's room. They must have talked all night. Then she'd smuggled him up breakfast. The adventure was going on without him. Romance was blooming up there in the attic. It was always the same, he thought. There was always some other guy. They were always a bit older, a bit cooler, had more stuff, and they always seemed to be so confident about everything. It had taken everything Jules had to ask Gen out, and now here was Theodore, hair like a neon sign, astonishing clothes, and his own time machine. If he wanted to go out with Gen, all he'd have to do was snap his fingers and it'd be on. Already, he'd just grabbed her hand, clicked on his remote, and away they'd gone. Jules didn't think his invitation to go to the movies, if she'd even heard it, was going to stack up against Theodore's dates. "Hey, Gen, like to go for a walk in the Hanging Gardens of Babylon? Want to go watch Mt. Everest being formed? Hey, I know, let's go to the T-Rex fight." Jules felt his earlier friendly feelings for Theodore being replaced by a slow-burning jealousy. Gen was his friend. They'd always been friends. Well, until recently anyway.

"Hey, I'm coming to school," announced Theodore brightly. "I'm going to be your cousin."

"Cousins? You and me?"

"Gen's idea. She said you're new, no one knows much about you. Cousin turns up for a day or two, has to come to school 'cause there's no one home. She said you'd be fine. We'll just bluff it out, no one's going to check."

Jules was really starting to dislike this morning. So Gen just thought of him as the new kid. Not a dear old friend. He wished he'd never gone away.

"Don't worry about it." Theodore was optimistic. "I'll fit right in."

Jules doubted that very much. Theodore was trying to blend in, but he remained a kid you would look twice at. In fact, probably three or four times. His hair was being normal—that is, it was being just one color, violet, although there was occasionally a faint red pulse at the roots. The Coat was being quiet and looked like a reasonably normal jacket, but underneath it Theodore was wearing a silver top and pants that were just too bright a green. His shoes, the purple shoes that took themselves on and off, were doing a reasonable impression of a pair of trainers, except they were trying just a bit too hard. They had stripes and swoops and reflector bits, and straps and air pumps and clear inserts and webbing and enormously huge soles and heels that flared out and seemed to cover about half the footpath. But then Jules shrugged. Who at school did look "normal"? He thought he did, but everyone else dyed their hair, shaved bits off, had piercings and bits of metal hanging off bits that probably didn't need it. There was a tattoo or two, and kids wore everything from high fashion to things they'd run up themselves and stapled together. Maybe Theodore will fit in just fine, he thought.

"Hi!"

Jules turned around to find Gen coming up behind them.

"Hi. Cousins?" he said, pointing at Theodore and raising his eyebrows.

"You could be cousins," said Gen defensively. "Got a better idea? He can't go home, he can't spend the day at my place, he can't be my cousin. You're new, no one's going to ask."

"You know, I'm not actually new. I used to live here."

"Yeah, but you went away. It's like you're new."

"Did you hide the JumpMan?" asked Theodore.

"Yep. No one'll find it," answered Gen.

Jules walked off in front of them, kicking at papers and stones in a particularly vindictive way.

They walked on like that for a while toward school, Jules out the front, hunched over, hands in pockets and Gen and Theodore deep in conversation behind him. Jules couldn't figure out which was worse: sulking along on his own, or missing out and not knowing what they were talking about. He chose the latter torment and dropped back to join them. As usual, he couldn't stay angry at Theodore for long. It was all just too fascinating and he kept getting swept up in it.

"Sure, I've seen dinosaurs," he was saying. "Dinosaur JumpSites are huge. There's the Baby Brachiosaurus Walk, the Dance of the Seventeen Stegosaurus, you can go swimming with Megalodon—they're like white pointers, only three times larger—Pterodactyl watching, they're all great."

Theodore rattled on for a while and when he stopped, Jules asked, "So you've got to go somewhere definite, right? You can't just go turn up any old place?"

"Well, nip. You could turn up somewhere three billion years ago and three seconds after you get there a volcano erupts right where you're standing," Theodore replied. "You go off to look at a war, or a beheading or something, and you don't want to be standing in the wrong place. Plenty of old TimeJumpers are missing a few bits. There was a kid only a few weeks ago, thought he'd visit the Indian Wars. I don't know if you know this but in a place called America, I think, there were these people living there and these other people came over and started fighting with them—"

"Yeah, we know about that," interrupted Gen. "What happened to the kid?"

"Oh right, well, he tried to find his own Site and bang, he turned up right in the path of an arrow."

"Is he all right?"

"He's got a pretty funny hole where his elbow should be. But he'll live."

"So how do you know where to go?" asked Jules.

"SiteSearchers."

"What are they?"

"Who are they," corrected Theodore. "Lunatics. Total zongoids. They pick a space–time coordinate and then they go there and fall out of the sky."

"What?"

"Well, the safest bet is to fall out of the sky toward the Earth. On the way down you can check if there's an earthquake, if you are about to land in the middle of some poisonous lake or whatever. They do some quick calculations and Jump straight back home. They keep doing that until they've narrowed down an actual Site."

"And then you can go there?"

"Yeah, well, if it's worth going to. In fifteen billion years of the history of the universe there's an awful lot of waiting around for something to happen. Finding those moments that are really spectacular is hard work. You want to go somewhere and watch some mud bubble up out of the ground, no problem. You want to go and see a T-Rex running down dinner or get a ringside seat at some jousting, that's a bit harder."

Jules was about to ask how come kids are just allowed to wander around history and what time do they have to be home, when Theodore disappeared again.

Gen screamed a little. "Where's he gone?"

Jules looked as dumbfounded as ever. "I don't know. I was just here, same as you. How would I know?"

"Well, he hasn't even got the JumpMan with him. How could he just go like that?"

It occurred to Jules that since Theodore had turned up, he'd been coming and going quite regularly.

"Gen, who knows? What do we know about him? Maybe the JumpMan got fixed and Jumped him out of here automatically. It's not like we've known him all that long." Not like me, he wanted to say. "Maybe he's not all that reliable. Maybe he's just gone."

"Yeah, right, Jules. I think I know him pretty well. I have just spent all night talking to him. I think he would have said good-bye if he wasn't coming back."

Jules went silent as jealously consumed him. It spread through his limbs like the flu. He ached with it. He hated the images that crawled into his brain and took root there, devouring his good mood like maggots. They'd talked all night? His worst fear. He'd have said "good-bye"? Not just "see you," or "later, dude"? But good-bye? His worst fear confirmed.

They plodded on in silence, Gen not offering anything further and Jules seething with shame and embarrassment at the things he imagined and the questions he wanted to ask but couldn't get out.

After about ten minutes of this, Theodore ran up behind them.

"Theodore! What happened, where did you go?"

And why didn't you stay there, thought Jules, hating the note of relief he heard in Gen's voice.

"Umm, can't really explain that," Theodore replied. "But it's going to be an interesting day."

"What do you mean?" asked Jules, but they were turning into the school gate and Theodore's whole face had lit up with eager curiosity at the prospect before them.

"Fantastic," he said. "Actually, this could be a great Site. An early third millennium school. What rubbish were they teaching then?"

Jules's school had once been Rosemount High but it was now referred to as the Southern Campus of the Multi Discipline Maxi Educational Facility Offering Both Vertical and Horizontal Integrated Learning Experiences for Years

Seven Through to University. At least that's what the Education Minister had called it when he was photographed in front of the gleaming new sign at the start of the year. Everyone else still called it Rosemount High.

Despite its optimistic new title, it was still a high school much like any other, a central two-story building built fifty years ago and now flanked by long, low additions added as the suburb had grown. The playing fields were surrounded by demountables, dropped there temporarily fifteen years ago.

Jules still felt apprehensive as he entered. This was the third year in a row he'd started a new school. He'd moved away with his mum and done Year Six at a new school. He'd started a new high school and done Year Seven there last year. Now he'd moved back with his dad and started Year Eight here. He was sick of feeling like he didn't quite belong. It wasn't the schoolwork that was hard to catch up with, that was easy enough. It was everything else that was confusing: who was cool and who wasn't; what you should eat at lunchtime; what kind of folders you should have; what kind of pens, pencils, calculator, and laptop were the best; what you could talk about; whether it was cool to play sports or music or just do nothing; and probably worst of all, what to wear.

The entrance hall door to the main building was propped

open by a garbage bin and the three of them walked in to be assaulted by the phenomenal noise of a few hundred kids on their way into class.

Voices yelling about nothing, voices chatting about everything, kids yelling for pens, paper, homework answers, excuses for homework, a seat with a friend. All the voices clanging up and down the long linoleum corridor, slapping off the metal lockers and ricocheting back and forth between the hard floor and the concrete ceiling above.

They immediately ran into Gen's girlfriends Sonja, Kyeela, and Bonnie, three heads from the four-headed monster, a phenomenal creature that knew everything that ever happened in any part of the school. The four-headed monster sucked in all the gossip and scandal through its eight ears. It had an opinion on everyone and everything and expressed it mainly by rolling its eight eyes back into its four heads in disbelief at how uncool, ignorant, and out of touch everyone was. Except for the monster, of course, and the one or two others it thought were OK.

"Gen, guess what—" Sonja started straight in and then stopped when she saw Jules.

"Jules. Hi." Kyeela said in a voice that suggested Gen and Jules had somehow got married overnight and now she better rush off and tell everyone else about it.

"Who's your new friend?" asked Bonnie, who'd had time

to take in Theodore's presence and was now looking him up and down, checking out every detail from the outlandish footwear to the hair, which was still largely violet but the little red flashes were now running through it like a line of tiny red fairy lights.

"Umm, cousin of Jules." Gen felt like a large neon sign had just been erected over her head. It read LIAR and there was an arrow pointing down at her.

"Yeah. His mum's sick and he's come to stay and Dad's at work so he had to come to school. It's all fixed up." Jules felt like he was on the stage at a school assembly and the school had just been asked to stand and yell LIAR at him.

Happily, Theodore provided the necessary distraction.

"Hi, everyone. So what's the local custom? Do newcomers have to greet the chief and drink goat's blood before being introduced to the rest of the tribe? Do I have to wrestle the village strongman? You know, where I come from, we've found introducing people to be a very effective way of getting to know people."

And then he stepped forward and started shaking hands with the girls.

"Hi, Theodore Pine. You can call me Theo. Eddie even, if you prefer. You're Bonnie? Charmed. Kyeela, that's unusual. Based on the cry of the dodo? No? It's exactly what it sounds like. KyEEEEELA. KyEEEEE-EEEEELA."

Theodore threw back his head and demonstrated. "And Sonja. Delightful. Do you know the Voyage of Queen Sonja? It's fantastic, totally boid, a very popular Site. Queen Sonja was a Norwegian Viking battle princess. When you get there, she's standing in the bow of the long-ship, sun glinting off her horns, and she's heading out to battle some lads from down the coast who want her cows very badly. Great battle. Oak, or rather, OK. So this is school? What's first class today, Destruction of the Species?"

Jules looked at the three girls and started laughing. This is what he and Gen must have looked like last night. The girls were standing with their mouths open, staring at Theodore. They stood transfixed, partly at what he was saying, but partly because as he said it, the red flashes through his violet hair had got very active and were now grooving away like there was a party going on up there.

Gen jumped forward, looked very determinedly at Theodore, and ran her fingers through her hair.

"Yes, sorry, Theodore. I guess we didn't have time to make the introductions like we didn't have time to do our *hair this morning*!"

Theodore's hair had taken off. A huge red sun was bursting on the crown of his head, and the tiny red flashes were running down his scalp like vigorous tadpoles. He was ignoring Gen's subtle attempts to get him to calm things down. He was staring up at the flag fluttering on top of the flagpole.

"Is that how you signal to one another? Do you fly that thing when there's disease about? No, I know, you're a nation state! That's your flag. Do you have your own money as well? Perhaps a song?"

Theodore looked around eagerly at the group who were regarding him with a range of reactions. Sonja still had the stupefied look, Kyeela had started to think he was cute, and Bonnie was looking sympathetic, as you would for a damaged person who was obviously in need of help and lengthy hospitalization. Gen and Jules were occupied in trying to distract Theodore from the flag and get him to do something about his hair.

He finally noticed them.

"Oh, oh, right. OK," he said, and his hair went immediately to a kind of muted grape, which did nothing to stop the girls from staring at it.

"Could you pay attention to a few things like that?" muttered Jules as they pulled him away from the girls and down the corridor. "Everyone noticed it."

"You know, remarkably in primitive societies you can show up and start turning Technicolor and if it's beyond their understanding, they will most likely ignore it."

"Hair color is not beyond those girls' understanding. They don't talk about much else," hissed Gen. "And stop observing everything and commenting all the time. You're at school. Just be a school kid. Have you ever been that?"

"Nip. Look, don't want to be a trouble, but your stairs aren't working."

Theodore was standing on the bottom stair, one hand on the banister and looking expectant.

"They're stairs, not an escalator," said Jules.

"Actual stairs? Oh, I thought you'd be over them. OK, I know how these work." And he promptly tripped up them.

Jules and Gen helped him up the stairs and steered him along the corridor to their first class. The bell had rung, the corridors were emptying, and they made it just in time, after Theodore had become fascinated with a padlock. "No Auto-Key? Surely you lose them all the time?," then a rubbish bin, and then crashed into the door after yelling "Open!" at it. "I didn't expect automatic movement sensors, but I thought it would respond to a clear command," he explained.

Eventually, under the stares of everyone, they ushered him to a desk.

Mr. Sims entered the classroom hard behind them.

"Morning, Class."

"Good morning, Mr. Sims."

"Now, the headmaster has asked me to announce that

afternoon sport is still going ahead, even though the weather looks against us right now. I'm sorry, I've had no word of a new student joining us. Who are you?"

"Theodore—"

"He's my cousin, sir!" Jules jumped up, hoping to stop an outburst from Theodore who was no doubt anxious to expand on the role of the teacher, the uselessness of chalk, and the design of the desks.

"Cousin?"

"Yes, sir. His mother's in the hospital and he's come to stay for a day or two and so we thought he better come to school. Dad phoned this morning."

"He did?"

Jules felt like he was getting better at lying now and hoped that none of the teachers during the day would remember to check with the headmaster about his cousin.

"All right, what's your name?"

"Theodore. Theodore Pine. You're going to teach all of us at once? Fascinating! How do you do it?"

"I beg your pardon?"

Here we go, thought Jules. Gen was looking equally apprehensive.

"You must be incredible! You can do a Learning Session with thirty students at a time? Woosh, none of our teachers ever attempt more than four."

Jules wondered if he should stage a diversion, but Mr. Sims was already interrupting Theodore.

"Yes, well, you're obviously very fortunate to go to such an institution. Thank you, ah . . ."

"Theodore."

"Yes, Theodore. All right then. Today in World History . . ."

When Mr. Sims said World History, Jules got a sinking feeling. He'd been focused on sneaking Theodore into class and hadn't thought about what that class was. Theodore had of course *been* to a lot of the world's history and would no doubt want to comment.

". . . I want to get you started on your major assignment for the rest of the term. It's largely about you doing your own research. I want you to discover how you would find out about a period in history that interests you. And so I want you to think about this question. If you could be anyone at all from any period in the past, who would you choose?"

Mr. Sims looked expectantly at the class. The class settled into its routine. The bright students noted down the question, underlined it, and started to think about it. The middle lot noted down the question and wondered if they'd be tested on it and hoped Mr. Sims wouldn't ask them for an answer right away. The bottom bunch gazed out the window and continued on with the elaborate doodles they'd begun three days before.

"Well?" asked Mr. Sims, as thirty students tried to look everywhere else but at him to avoid being the first to answer. "If you could be anyone you like in the entire history of the world, who would you be?"

"Kylie Minogue!" piped up Harry Fleming, who could always be relied upon to come up with an opening gag.

"Britney Spears!" tried Dominic Moore, who would always do whatever Harry Fleming was doing. And that inspired the others.

"Brad Pitt!"

"Russell Crowe!"

"Nicole Kidman!"

"Ricky Martin!"

"David Beckham!"

"Shaquille O'Neil!"

Mr. Sims nodded and smiled. At their age he would have yelled out "Frida" from Abba. That would have been embarrassing. He'd let them get through their list of favorite celebrities. Couple of the smart kids would join in soon and bring them back around.

"Christopher Columbus." There was one now.

"Sir Isaac Newton." Give that girl an apple!

"Jack the Ripper." What? Mr. Sims located the boy who'd spoken up. Quiet lad, never said much. Must mention it to the school psychologist. He started calming the class down.

"OK, OK. You're beginning to get the general idea." And then he noticed Theodore who was sitting in his desk smirking to himself. Strange boy, thought Mr. Sims.

"What is it, Theodore? This amusing you?"

"Oh, well, this was a very popular game for a while, but then we came up with the answer."

"*The* answer?' said Mr. Sims. 'It's not a question that has only one answer. You can be anybody you want, everyone has a different answer."

"Nip. Eventually everyone came up with the same answer. The best thing you can possibly be out of all possibilities, and it just squeezes out Roman Emperor, Impressionist Painter in Paris, or Assyrian Goat Herder With The Most Goats—the best thing to be is High Priest in Tahiti any time in Mil 1. It's fantastic."

Mr. Sims had his mouth open as though he would like to speak but had no idea what to say. Jules recognized the expression as one that had been on his face a fair bit since last night. Theodore had stood up and started to pace around the classroom.

"The High Priest. Everyone loves him," he continued. "He has the last word on everything, he gets a nice place to live in, people heat up baths for him, he gets the best breadfruit and mango and fish delivered every lunchtime. And it's in Tahiti! Most beautiful place in the world with the best weather. Perfect! And you know why he gets all this?"

Theodore paused and looked around. The class was staring at him and so absorbed in what he was saying, they all shook their heads. Mr. Sims looked on, astonished. Good grief, he thought. Weird little kid's got all of them listening. I can never do that.

"Because the High Priest is the one who knows when the next solar eclipse is." Theodore slapped his hands in triumph. "Every couple of years he starts muttering about how the gods are going to eat the Sun! And then he mutters a bit louder, 'But don't worry, I can save us! I will rescue the Sun!' He builds a big fire, sticks a lot of parrot feathers behind his ears, and starts dancing around. The sky goes dark, everyone else hits the dirt, but he stands up there, old oyster shells around his neck, big staff carved from a washed-up whalebone, and demands that the gods give back the Sun. Of course, what happens? Eclipse finishes, Sun comes back, all the locals think he saved the Sun! All the men give him their pot of best fermented pineapple juice, all the dusky maidens start dropping by with sweet potato pie. It's fantastic!"

Theodore beamed at them all.

"The only thing anyone has ever found that's even remotely like it is being a rock star near the end of Mil 2. That's a close second, but you have to write songs and hang out with models and actors. So that's the answer, pretty much. Tahitian High Priest. Why would you want to be anything else?"

Mr. Sims's eyes narrowed. This boy with the strange jacket had just ruined the assignment. He felt an entire term's work slipping away from him. He had to save it.

"All right, thank you, Theodore. That's very interesting. Now why don't we all take a few minutes to jot down any other ideas we might have. Unlike our new friend Theodore here, I don't happen to think there's only one answer to that question, so let's see if we can think of some others."

The class looked puzzled, and only the boy who wanted to be Jack the Ripper turned his attention to his books. He began writing in very small, almost illegible handwriting about what he'd like to do to a High Priest if he found him on the streets of London in 1890.

Mr. Sims came over and sat on Theodore's desk.

"Umm, Theodore. What school do you normally go to?"

Jules stood up and fainted.

"Santorini!" said Mr. Sims. "Are you all right?" He leapt off the desk and crouched next to Jules. Jules moaned a little. Gen jumped up from her desk.

"Sir! His mother said we were to take him to sick bay straightaway if this happened."

"She did?" Mr. Sims had the feeling that everything was starting to slip away from him.

"Yes, sir. Maybe Theodore could give me a hand."

"Ahh, yes all right." The boy was interesting but perhaps it would be better to get him out of there before he came up with some way of ruining the entire year's work.

Gen and Theodore helped Jules to his feet and headed out the door.

"What the hell is wrong with you?" Out in the corridor, Jules was suddenly well again. "What happened to 'Don't Touch Anything'? Why don't you just stand up there and tell everyone about TimeJumping? I thought no one was meant to know."

"This is just too amazing!" said Theodore, laughing. "I thought TimeJumping and being invisible was good, but being visible and being in something, participating, that's just, well, amazing!"

Theodore was giggling and dancing around when The Coat suddenly spoke up. And it wasn't speaking in the friendly voice-over style that it usually employed.

"This is an official announcement. Monitoring of recordings begun 17.25 hours ago indicate an almost constant breach of the TimeCode. Record function will remain on. Recording will be viewed by Code Cops on TimeJumper's return. Further breaches could lead to a loss of Jump

Licence or punishment. Please keep in mind that there is One Rule And One Rule Only. Don't Touch Anything!"

Theodore stopped dancing when he heard the announcement.

The Coat continued, now in a smoother tone. "In trouble? Call 1-800-T I M E L A W—"

"Yeah, thanks, Coat."

Theodore looked troubled. "What do they expect me to do? I'm visible here in Mil 3. Do they think I should hide in a cupboard? I'm not doing anything. Nothing's going wrong."

Gen led them out into the quadrangle and they sat on a bench where they couldn't be seen.

"I don't know what you should do, Theodore, but you keep telling us not to tell anyone, and we're meant to be hiding you and all you do is jump up and down and yell, Look at me, I'm from the future!"

Theodore nodded.

"Yip, you're right. I'll try."

They sat in silence for a while.

"Has anyone ever come back and tried to change things?" asked Jules.

"Oh, there's been a couple," said Theodore. "Early TimeJumpers used to get seen all the time."

"Really?"

"See, on the early units, you'd set the time–space coordinates and they wouldn't just Jump you there. You had to pass through the time and the space. Sometimes as you passed through, you'd flicker into view for a moment, sometimes longer. The JumpMan was checking coordinates and would bring you into full view for a moment. Anyway, you'd flicker into view, someone would see you and they'd freak out, and then you'd disappear again. Go back a hundred years and you might flicker into view again. The locals would start to talk. Think the place was haunted or something."

"Ghosts?" said Gen. "You mean ghosts are really Time-Jumpers?"

"See the problem?" Theodore nodded. "Even just being seen for a second or two, and you've suddenly got every-one believing in ghosts. No one thought that'd happen. Like I said, now you two know about everything. Who knows how that might change stuff for you, in your future."

Theodore sat there chewing his lip and looking a bit worried about everything. Jules and Gen, their minds lost in thought, tried to understand what Theodore was telling them. It was astonishing the way Theodore seemed to live with time travel and all its complexities and paradoxes without any more effort than they lived with the road rules. In Theodore's world, all time was just a moment away. The billions of years of existence of the universe didn't worry him at all.

"Leon Derwent was one," said Theodore after a while.

"One what?" asked Gen.

"One who came back and got stuck. He didn't mean to but he got trapped in Renaissance Italy. He wandered around, tried to explain helicopters to everyone, how the human body worked, and he wasn't a bad painter either. He took up a local identity, da Vinci I think it was, and did quite well."

"Leonardo da Vinci?" asked Jules.

"Right. Heard of him, have you? Yip, well, by the time everyone realized what had happened, there was no getting him back, he was too famous. They sent Code Cops back to fabricate a history for him and it appears to have worked. Bill Gates was another one."

"Bill Gates is from the future?"

Theo nodded. "Bill Gates was a total delinquent. He stole his father's JumpMan and managed to arrive late second millennium just as computers were getting going. He took one look around, patented the operating system, and cleaned up."

"He's still cleaning up."

"He's still around? That's interesting."

"He's the richest man in the world."

"Well, in our time, he's just a very naughty boy."

The bell rang, and Jules and Gen stood up.

"Do you think you can shut up for the rest of the morning, or do I have to faint in every class?" asked Jules.

"Don't worry. I'll behave."

He didn't.

In Mathematics, Theodore filled the board with equations and told hilarious tales about life at home with Pythagoras. In Geography he got into a screaming match with the teacher arguing that global warming was nothing to worry about and in English he was quiet for a while, but then he started crying as Mrs. Stengard read out *Romeo and Juliet*.

Mrs. Stengard got them to read on their own and Theodore was finally silent, totally absorbed, although he did keep muttering, "I have to take this back, it's a new Shakespeare."

The morning passed. Theodore was acting out the death of Romeo to himself while Jules and Gen were pretending to work but were mainly just sitting there worrying that Theodore's hair would suddenly start grooving away again, or that The Coat would stop being a normal kind of jacket and try to arrest him, when the headmaster's secretary peered around the door. Her glasses were half falling off her nose and her hair had come adrift from its usual tight arrangement. She looked flustered and was pulling at her clothes like it was suddenly very hot.

It was usual to knock and ask to be admitted into a classroom, but the secretary barged in, pointed at Jules and Gen, and in a voice loud and hysterical, demanded, "Genevieve Corrigan and Jules Santorini, the headmaster's office, now. Right now. Right? Now." She turned and stormed off in the wrong direction toward the windows, came to an abrupt halt, screamed a little, and then headed back toward the door.

Genevieve and Jules rose, and Theodore stood up with them.

Sally-Anne Priestley, the secretary usually known as the Wardress, stopped and pointed at Theodore.

"Who are you?" she screeched. "What do you think you're doing?"

Jules spoke up. "He's my cousin. He's just visiting. If I have to go somewhere, he better come too."

Normally the Wardress would have had Theodore marching back to his seat with a glare and a sneer, but today she simply turned, stumbled on her high heels, recovered, and then fired off a most un-Wardress-like "Whatever," before marching out the door and slamming it closed in front of the three of them.

In the corridor, Theodore drew them in close.

"Remember I said it was going to be an interesting day? Well, it starts now. Look, ah, when we get in there, don't freak out. Secondly, don't draw attention to me. Thirdly, Jules, as soon as you can, distract everyone's attention from me and Gen's mother, or one of Gen's mothers at least. And fourthly—"

Jules hoped fourthly wasn't all that important since they were now being ushered into Mr. McGeoghan's office and Theodore was unable to explain any further. Jules and Gen looked at each other and then Gen looked away and exclaimed, "Mum, what are you doing . . . here . . ."

Her voice trailed off as she started to do exactly what Theodore had told her not to.

She freaked out. She screamed for a bit and then started to whimper like a fretful puppy.

Jules supposed that that was because there were two Katherine Corrigans in the headmaster's office. One was lying on the couch, occasionally raising her head and looking at the other one who was sitting gibbering in the corner. "I'm at home. I'm at home. I can't be looking at me. It's Genevieve. Something happened last night. I know. I know. She's gone strange. I must be at home. That can't be me. Or I can't be me. But I'm me. Who else can I be but who I am? Hahhhahaha." And she dissolved into giggles that were nervous in a way you usually don't hear outside of armed hold-ups or hostage situations.

Back on the couch, the other Katherine Corrigan was starting to whine a little and spray spittle around the room. Jules stood stock still and then started doing at least two of the things Theodore had asked them not to do. He freaked out and he drew attention to Theodore.

"Theodore," he hissed. "Theo. Look. Is this something to do with you?"

Theodore looked at him like he was a very annoying small child and Jules eventually shut up. But he didn't stop freaking out.

There was much to be freaked out about. There were two Katherine Corrigans in the room and they both appeared to be helping each other up a spiral of battiness, but the Katherine in the corner also had the JumpMan. She held the red remote in one hand and clutched the sphere to her chest with the other, dragging her fingers across it with such force that she'd already broken two of her nails.

Jules looked around the room. As well as the double mums, himself, Gen, and Theodore, the headmaster was there at his desk. Mr. McGeoghan was attempting to be a picture of calm and control in the middle of this chaos, but he didn't seem to know what to do, and so he was doing many things at once. He was taking off his jacket. He was putting it back on. He was pulling at his tie. He was picking up the phone and putting it down again and saying things like, "Water. Hot towels. I'll call an ambulance. Perhaps a priest. Sandwiches. Should I call the department?"

Theodore needn't have worried. Jules could have jumped on the desk, rung a large bell, taken off his clothes, and shouted, "Theodore's here!" and no one would have noticed. The doubling of Gen's mum was the main attraction in this room. Theodore had realized this and was now walking calmly around the room to the Katherine in the corner.

Genevieve was trying to help the Katherine on the couch, but Sally-Anne Priestley, the Wardress, was standing on a chair right next to her announcing things.

"Thank you. Thank you everybody. One thing at a time. Now, we've got a situation but I'm sure if we take it one thing at a time, it'll all make sense. The other women from the cafeteria and Mr. Croker are in the sick bay. They all claim that Katherine Corrigan appeared on the table in the cafeteria clutching that silver ball thing while Katherine Corrigan was making fruit salad." Her voice was cracking up. "Our next priority must be Mrs. . . . ah, Mrs. . . ." and she looked from one Katherine Corrigan to the other and then moaned a little before getting down from the chair, sitting on it, and starting to weep.

This was all too much for Genevieve, whose knees had

given way and she was now slumped on the couch next to her mother. Or one of her mothers. She was massaging this mother's ankle like she was trying to unscrew it and looking from this mother to that mother with a look that said things better get back to normal in about five seconds or I'm going to start wailing like everyone else in here.

Mr. McGeoghan had his head in his hands and was muttering, "I have to ring the Minister. I can't ring the Minister. I have to ring the Minister. I can't ring the Minister."

Jules had started to get a dim sense of some connection between what was going on here and Theodore's disappearance this morning. He didn't understand the connection but it did help him to concentrate and through the wailing and the tugging at ties and the general hysteria, he saw Theodore trying to get his attention.

Distraction time.

This wasn't going to be easy. Everyone in the room was pretty much focused on losing their grip.

All he could think of was a classified ad his dad had shown him once. Tony had thought the ad was pretty funny. He had to do something.

"Sex!" he shouted.

No one paid any attention.

"Sex!" he shouted again.

People don't usually yell out the word "sex," and in

almost any other gathering doing so would have swung all eyes on to the speaker, but this was a tough room. Identical mothers is hard to top.

"Sex!" he screamed. "Sex sex sex sex SEEEEEXXXXXX!"

Silence. Everyone was staring at him.

"OK," he said, "now I've got your attention—" And that was long enough for Theodore. He grabbed the remote from the clenched grip of Genevieve's mum, pointed it at the sphere, pressed the large central button, and . . .

The morning passed. Theodore was acting out the death of Romeo to himself while Jules and Gen were pretending to work but were mainly just sitting there worrying that Theodore's hair would suddenly start grooving away again, or that The Coat would stop being a normal kind of jacket and try to arrest him.

Theodore leaned across and nudged Jules. "Gen," he whispered as well and Gen turned around.

"Umm, in a little under a minute, you're going to experience something really horrible. It's called a Rewind," said Theodore. "It's about as pleasant as being violently seasick while you're lying in the bath. We've actually jumped back to this moment from seven and a half minutes in the future and we're about to go through those seven and a half minutes again. You won't actually go anywhere, but in order to get time back into balance, you've got to live through the time as you would have if you hadn't gone and done something else. This is what happens when you Rewind. I mean, you know, you can't just go adding time to the universe any more than you can subtract it, so you can kind of go back and erase things but then you've got to balance it up. Uh-oh, it's starting."

Theodore fell back into his chair, and Jules felt like his head had been torn off. Half of him seemed to be looking at Theodore and then going back to his schoolwork. The other half was experiencing the events of the last seven and half minutes but in reverse. Theodore wasn't snatching the remote away from Katherine, it looked like he was thrusting it back into her hand. Then he walked calmly backward as Jules jumped off the chair after yelling "XES" a few times.

He felt like he'd been tied to two bolting horses heading off in opposite directions. His head ached, and he felt certain that he would soon be throwing up.

Everything that had happened since the Wardress came and got him was rewinding through while he simultaneously sat here in class and did what he would have done if that had never happened.

He managed to look around at Theodore who was looking green from the hair down, and over to Gen who was gently banging her head on the desk while she bit her biro in half.

Mrs. Stengard came over.

"Jules."

Jules turned his eyeballs in her direction. They felt like they'd been glued into his head and were not meant to move.

"Hgrhhmmm?" he managed.

"How are you settling in?"

Jules heard the question but at the same time he was experiencing walking into the headmaster's office and seeing the two mums for the first time only backward and so although he wanted to reply, "Fine. Just fine, thanks," he found himself saying,

"Sclog, phring sclog, mrrrggghhhehe."

"I just wanted to check if you were feeling like you were keeping up with everything?"

"Ga. Ga. Gaarcksrk. Ga. Sure," he said.

"Are you all right?" Mrs. Stengard looked concerned.

"Fa. Frgkckr. Fine," he replied.

"Well, if you need any extra help, make sure you ask for it, OK?"

Jules nodded, amazed he hadn't been sick all over her.

His brain was now threatening permanent separation and demanding they go and see someone, a counselor, a therapist.

In the Rewind, Jules, Theodore, and Gen were now walking backward into the classroom. Jules came and sat down with himself. The past movements and the present were only slightly out of phase and Jules felt an enormous pressure at his temples. He felt like he was screaming in the back of his throat. There was a huge rushing of air around his ears, and then bang, it all stopped.

He grabbed the side of his desk to steady himself and gulped in air, looking around warily as though any moment something equally disturbing was going to happen.

The bell rang and he jumped out of his skin.

They dragged themselves out of their desks and staggered to the door.

"Jules," called Mrs. Stengard.

"Yes?" he said weakly.

"Don't forget, if it's all getting too much, come and see me."

Jules waved wanly and headed out the door.

Meanwhile . . .

DUNCAN NOONG SAT FORWARD IN EXCITEMENT. The last time he'd done that had been . . . had been . . . well, it was a very long time ago. Not a lot of excitement in the life of a TimeKeeper. Vital work, but dreadfully dull. No one ever wanted to talk to him.

"What do you do, they'd ask." For a while he'd pretended he did something else. For a few years he mumbled it. Now he said it loudly, a bit aggressively, and dared them to make their feeble jokes.

"I'm a TimeKeeper," he'd say. "Bureau of Universal Chronology."

"Oh, yip?" they'd say politely. "Bet you're never late."

Why did they all think they were the first to say it?

And then they went back to talking to someone more interesting. If only they knew. They all thought it meant wearing an old brown jacket and shuffling about looking at clocks. They all thought you had to want to be bored.

A real Moon spotter, to do that kind of work.

But it was beautiful work. There was time ticking away in front of him. On his shift in the dead of night, which he worked alone, he was the sole witness of AllTime. Well, him and the station's pet armadillo.

And occasionally, he'd do the calculations to keep time in balance. That's why he was leaning forward in excitement.

Someone was doing a Rewind. But they were doing it in a time no one was meant to be.

chapter five

Time and Time Again

Gen's mum was in the cafeteria with the other mothers and one father. It was Parents' Day in the cafeteria, and everything was almost normal. The mothers were making sandwiches, but would then squirt sauce into them like they were pies. The father was taking orders from the kids and then he'd forget them, and then ask them again like he'd never heard the orders in the first place. Then he'd come back with three cream buns instead of a chicken roll and an apple.

Katherine Corrigan was chopping up fruit salad but not very well. She'd chop a banana in half and then throw it into the bowl. As they stood in the queue watching her, she sliced an orange into quarters and threw that in the bowl. She hadn't peeled it. She looked at Theodore for a little too long, Jules thought, but he was too hungry to care.

"I'm starving," said Gen.

"Me too," said Jules.

"It's the Rewind," said Theodore. "Takes it out of you."

"What happened?" asked Gen.

"I'll order," said Jules, "you two go and get a table. Don't start explaining anything without me."

Theodore and Gen headed off to find a table. Jules ordered.

"Six pies, six ham and cheese sandwiches, and three big cartons of chocolate milk please."

Jules repeated the order three times and the father came back with some pizza slices, several quiches, orange juice, and some apples.

Jules took it and went to find the other two.

"What do you call this?" Theodore bit a little off a pizza slice.

"Pizza."

"Woosh, this stuff is great." Theodore scoffed it down.

The Coat sprang into action.

"Automatic override of Mute function," it announced. "Theodore, must advise that again you are taking in food-stuffs with little or no nutritional value. High fat content, dangerous levels of melted yellow stuff, and a kind of preserved spiced meat that is made with all sorts of bits of animal—"

"Shut up, Coat!" Theodore yelled and several kids at other tables looked around. Jules noticed there was a fair bit of pointing at Theodore going on. Gossip about him was whipping around the room. No one talked about me on my first day, thought Jules gloomily.

"What happened in there?" asked Gen again.

"Oh, the Rewind?"

"The Rewind, my two mothers, the whole thing, thank you."

"She found the JumpMan."

"Mum did?"

"Uh-huh. She pressed the remote and I don't really know how, but it Jumped her about two hours into the future. But it also left herself in the present. One self has gone into the future, while the other self tidies up the house and gets ready and drives over to the cafeteria and then meets itself arriving from the past."

"It can do that? You can go and meet yourself?"

"Not normally. And when people do, they never like

what they see," explained Theodore. "You're not meant to do that sort of stuff with a JumpMan. But this one, it does some strange stuff."

"And everyone else could see this?" said Gen.

"Of course. Big panic. We all end up in the headmaster's office."

"So what happened after I started yelling?" asked Jules.

"Did you yell out 'Sex'?" asked Gen.

"Yes."

"Is that a thirteen-year-old boy thing?"

"Shut up, Gen, it's all I could think of. You grabbed the remote, then what happened?" Jules was keen to move the story along.

"I pressed Undo," said Theodore. "Jumped back with your mum to the cafeteria and pressed Undo again to get back to the moment she picked up the JumpMan. Instead of her pressing the button I started a Rewind."

"Did Mum find the JumpMan just after we left for school?"

"Exactly. That's when I disappeared this morning. I was pulled forward into the Undo Jumps and then ended up back at Gen's place. That's when I ran up behind you as we were walking here."

Jules felt like he was understanding Theodore's story but he knew now that as soon as he felt like that, he was about to be completely confused again. He tried a question.

"So you went into the future to rewind the past to catch up with the present we would have had if we hadn't had had that future?"

Theodore leaned across and shook his hand.

"Couldn't have put it less clearly myself. I really think you're getting the hang of it, Jules. Can you have three 'hads' in a row like that in a sentence? 'Hadn't had had'? Is that a record?"

"Did everyone go through Rewind, like we did?" asked Gen.

"The entire universe did, but it's all relative really. Depends on your proximity to the central event. You, me, Jules, your mum got the worst of it. The galaxy down the road probably didn't notice much."

"So they all know. They'll know something weird's going on." Gen looked over at the parents serving in the cafeteria. The queue was now stretching back to the door as the father taking orders was staring at a ten dollar note like he'd never seen it before.

"Well, they're all a bit disorientated. But it makes no sense to them, so they'll soon reject it as some kind of dream. They'll think it's something they ate," said Theodore, picking up an apple.

"So why don't we feel like that?"

"Because there's us. The three of us confirm one another's memory and experience of what happened. And I'm here to explain it. Imagine going through this morning without me? Do you think your headmaster could even begin to tell someone else what he thinks happened in his office? He'll just take the rest of the day off. Ha!"

Theodore let out a sudden explosion of laughter.

"I don't believe it!" he shouted. "Applesticker! There's a little sticker on the apple. It's an applesticker!"

Theodore looked at them with the biggest grin on his face.

"Don't you get it?" He peeled off the sticker and showed them, laughing at it as he did so. Jules and Gen didn't get it.

"We have this saying, right? 'As stupid as applestickers.' It's just something people say. If you think someone's an idiot, you call them an applesticker." Jules recalled that Theodore had called him that last night. "But no one ever knew what it actually meant. It's so Mil 3, isn't it? You put a little sticker on every apple? Why? It's an apple!" Theodore laughed like this was the funniest thing in the world.

"Hi, Jules," said someone slipping into the seat next to him. Jules turned away from the chuckling Theodore. Sitting next to him was Max. Max Pierera. One time great mate, now Max was in a kind of gang. Or rather, with four other guys who thought they were a gang. They swaggered around like they'd spent the night stealing cars, smoking cigarettes and doing deals, and involved in secret gang stuff, when everyone knew they'd actually been at home, worked on their assignments, kissed their mums, and then gone to beddy-byes right on time. Jules didn't really want to be in the gang, but he missed being mates with Max. And it was Max who'd dared him to ask Gen out. And to get her to bring Sonja, because he wanted to go out with her. Jules sighed. Was this his life or was he in a daytime television show?

"Gen," said Max, nodding hello and smirking. "Who's the new dude?" Max squirted a thin stream of spit at the floor. This was one of his tough things.

That's disgusting, thought Jules. Jules introduced Theodore who got up and started to go around the tables picking up other bits of fruit.

"Bananastickers!" he yelled at them and laughed.

Max frowned a little but then returned to the scheme at hand.

"So, what are you up to Friday night? Any plans?" Max leaned forward with a suggestive grin on his face.

"Umm, well, you know how it is. I don't want to be tied down too early," said Jules. "Lot of things I could be doing. What about you?"

Max just laughed and got up from the table.

"I don't know," he said. "Probably just stay home and eat chicken."

He flapped his arms and clucked softly and walked away.

Jules watched him go. Was it worth it? Was he only asking Gen out because of Max? Well, yes, he thought, because he didn't really want to ask her out. All he really wanted was for them to be friends again, like they used to be, but that didn't seem to be possible, so he guessed he'd just have to take her out. Not that he'd mind taking her out because he really did like her and now that he was back, well, she really was quite attractive. "Attractive"—that was the kind of word your auntie used. He thought she was really pretty. Beautiful. He wanted to . . . to . . .

~ *Wow! said his brain. You're having a lot of trouble with the boy/girl stuff, aren't you?*

~ *Yes, he thought, hoping his brain would be sympathetic.*

~ *You can't even admit to yourself what you really want.*

~ *I don't know what I really want, said Jules. Anyway, where have you been all morning?*

~ *Oh, I was there. But I couldn't help you much.*

Jules smiled a bit and then realized that he was now

sitting alone with Gen. He had been for a while. She was looking at him with something that might be a smile or perhaps she just wanted to be sick. How do you ever know? he thought.

~ *You don't, said his brain.*

Jules thought, I'll try again. I'll ask her out. He took a deep breath just as Theodore threw himself back into the chair opposite him. On the end of his fingers were stickers from every possible fruit.

"No one likes them!" he chortled. "No one knows why you need stickers on fruit, and everyone finds them annoying. Mil 3 is so funny!"

Jules let out an exasperated sigh.

Gen moaned. "I want to go home. I feel terrible."

"Yip, your first Rewind. It'll take a while."

The bell rang for the end of lunch. They dragged themselves off. The afternoon passed slowly and nothing much happened. Even Theodore managed to be quiet for most of the time, apart from a couple of asides in Biology about DNA reconstruction. When the bell rang at the end of the day they gratefully headed home.

Theodore wanted to go and check on the JumpMan. Jules needed to eat and clean up.

"Come over later," said Gen, smiling at him as they reached his front gate. Jules's spirits soared. That was an actual invitation. He resisted skipping until they were out of sight.

Jules lay on the couch. Usually he'd start flicking around channels until he got bored and then he'd go and start his homework. His dad'd be home about five-thirty and then they'd clean up the kitchen together and cook dinner. Jules hoped for takeaway. His dad was determined to deliver a nutritious diet, as all the books said this was important. The kitchen was full of grains, pulses, brown rice, and vegetables. Neither of them knew how to combine them into something they'd actually want to eat. So they ate a lot of Thai takeaway, a lot of pizza, and a lot of breakfast cereal.

Today Jules lay there, his mind trying to catch up with the recent activity. Theodore said he was from three thousand years in the future. Last night Gen had gone back four thousand years to the building of the Great Pyramid. Today Gen's mother had leapt forward two hours in the future. To Theodore this time that he, Jules, was living in was the past. To Jules it was now, and it was Theodore who was from the future. Was there a future after Theodore? A time still farther on, that was even more incredible? Where was the past? Where was it kept? How could the past be still going on right now? Did people in the past keep living it over and over again? If Gen's mother could go two hours into the future, could he go two hours into the past? Could he go back and look at himself in school this afternoon? Could he go back one minute? Or forward?

He started to doze off, exhausted from everything that had been happening, when his brain woke him up again playing with a whole new question.

~ *When was the present?*

"The present," he said out loud, "is now."

~ *Oh now, is it? said his brain. But as soon as you said "now," it was past.*

~ *Yes, but, we're still in the present, aren't we?*

~ *Are we? That "now" you said is now ten seconds ago. It's in the past, argued his brain. So the present is now.*

~ *Now?*

~ *Too late, it's already past.*

Jules could swear his brain gave a triumphant snigger.

~ *Well OK, brain, you're so smart, when is the present?*

~ *Beats me. Everything's starting to seem like the past.*

Jules rubbed his eyes and headed to the bathroom to have a shower. He'd always felt that time was something that was continually moving forward but as he walked through the house to the bathroom, he started to see time as something that flowed away from him, leaving a long trail of "nows" behind him. As soon as you tried to grab on to the present, it turned immediately into the past.

So when is the future? he thought as he turned on the shower and watched the water fall from the faucet. As well as the past trailing along behind him like a vapor trail from a jet, he was always taking one step into the future.

As he stepped into the shower, Jules made a prediction. In a second, I will reach forward and grab the soap. There. He grabbed the soap. For the tiniest instant the future became the present and then as he began to soap his chest and his arms, it became the past.

He held his head under the water for a long time, but nothing became clearer. Then he became very still. If I do nothing, then I'm constantly in the present. Time flows past me. It's the same as the water in the shower. But then time isn't outside of me, like the water is. He felt a strange kind of vacuum enter him. Perhaps I'm never in the present, he thought. I'm only ever somewhere between the future and the past. And that moment is so short that it never exists.

~ Very profound, commented his brain.

~ Yes, but does it mean anything? Jules asked.

~ Sounds like it does. "I'm the meat in a sandwich of the future and the past." Should put that on a T-shirt.

~ Thanks, brain. Are you ever helpful?

~ Constantly.

He got out and dried himself, then headed upstairs for some clean clothes. He wanted to wear something cool. Being around Theodore's Coat and shoes and constantly adapting wardrobe made him feel drab. He came back downstairs just as his dad walked in through the front door.

"Jules? You here?"

"In the kitchen, Dad."

"G'day, how are you? You're all cleaned up. Going out, mate?"

"Yeah, well, had a bit of a big day. But yeah, I might go over to Gen's? Do some more work on that assignment."

"Uh-huh."

Jules could see his dad processing that bit of information and trying to figure out a response.

"Homework?"

"Uh-huh."

"Up in her room?"

"I suppose so. That's where she studies, I guess."

"Uh-huh," Tony said again.

Tony turned his attention to preparing noodles and stir-fried veggies. Oh no, he thought. Do I have to have a little talk with Jules? Do we have to do the father and son thing? Surely Jules and Gen aren't up in the bedroom . . . They're only thirteen. Hang on, she's nearly fourteen. What had he been doing at that age? Tony stopped slicing beans as memory flooded in. He turned and faced Jules.

"Mate. If you and Gen . . . Or I mean more, are you and Gen, umm, I mean, not that's anything wrong, it's all normal, mate. But you know, if you and Gen . . . you know."

Tony dried up and realized he was standing at the kitchen sink wearing an apron, holding a carving knife in one hand, and nodding at his thirteen-year-old son who had a carefully neutral look on his face.

"Well, you could talk about it, right?"

"Sure, Dad." Jules gave him a half smile and disappeared out into the lounge.

Yep, well handled, thought Tony. Really got the communication going there. I'm sure Jules feels like he can come and talk to me anytime about anything. Boys. Why can't they stay about seven forever?

Twenty minutes later, dinner was ready. Tony called Jules in. They sat and ate in silence that was midway between companionable and awkward. When they finished, Tony put down his fork and looked at his son.

"When I was thirteen and a half, I was in love with Wendy Melville. One night at a birthday party for one of her friends, we kissed. For an hour and a half. I mean literally, an hour and a half. I leaned forward and kissed, and it was an hour and a half before I came up again. Both of us were too terrified to move. She dumped me the next day. A couple of weeks later, I was on the golf course, caddying for my dad. On the fourteenth, he turned to me and said, 'We don't have to have the father-and-son talk, do we? You know all the birds and bees and baby stuff, right?' My father looked up the fairway and squinted against the light. 'It all starts with kissing, you know,' said my dad, kind of half to himself. 'Five iron, I reckon from here.'"

Jules's mouth was hanging open. He was embarrassed and it felt like he was blushing from the backs of his knees up to the roots of his hair. But he'd never heard his dad talk like this either.

"I was seventeen before I kissed a girl again. Years of torture. You need to talk to me, Jules, I'm here, mate. I know this stuff is embarrassing and awkward and you want me to shut up, and don't worry, I will. But I just want you to know, you start feeling a bit out of your depth, you can talk to me."

Jules nodded but didn't trust his voice to work. He could feel a little tingling in his eyes like he wanted to cry. Maybe being back here with his dad wouldn't be too bad.

"Go on, off you go. What time will you be back?"

"Nine-thirty?" asked Jules.

"That's plenty late enough for a school night. No later. I'm trusting you, mate. See you here, nine-thirty."

Jules got up, found his backpack, and headed out the

door. Tony picked up the plates, dropped them in the sink, and then started laughing. That was awful. He was going to have to think about this. There had to be a better way.

Gen's front door was wrenched open almost as soon as Jules rang the bell. It was Cynthia standing there.

"You're back. Mum keeps talking about you. I reckon you and Gen are doing it. You guys are being so weird and now Mum's gone mad too. You're doing it, aren't you?"

What was it with everyone? Couldn't a boy and girl spend a couple of evenings together without everyone thinking they were on?

~ *No, said his brain. Human nature. If you're five years old, then boys and girls playing together is cute. If you're eight, then boys and girls don't play together because they think the other is stinky and full of germs. If you're thirteen, there's no more playing. You're boyfriend and girlfriend.*

~ *Shut up, brain, said Jules. I just want—*

But Jules couldn't really pretend to himself anymore. He did want to be Gen's boyfriend. And that wasn't going to happen with Theodore around.

Jules looked down at Cynthia, as the evil grin spread across her tiny face. She looked like a kind of miniature demon. Katherine came to the door and stood behind her.

"Jules! You! It's always you! Tell me what's going on. Something happened today. Ever since you came for dinner something's been happening! Come inside! Now!"

Katherine was in her dressing gown and holding it tightly across her. Her eyes were wide and unblinking. In one hand she held a wineglass from which she kept taking nervous little sips even though the glass was now empty. She pulled Jules inside, all but wrenching his arm from its socket.

"What are you doing here?" Her hand remained clamped around his wrist. She pulled Jules up close to her and stared right into his eyes.

"Homework?" ventured Jules.

"Homework!" Katherine snorted. "Why are you two so keen on homework all of a sudden? You turn up to do homework and things start going crazy. It was crazy at the cafeteria and you were there. I was in the headmaster's office and you were there again! Now here you are and I want to know what's going on."

Jules's wrist started to ache, and he tried to break off Katherine's piercing gaze.

"Mrs. Corrigan, there's nothing going on. It's just homework." Jules hoped he sounded convincing.

"Something's going on!" Katherine hissed at him.

"Genevieve won't come down from her room. You're here again. You make me nervous."

She let go of his arm to clutch at the front of her dressing gown and took another nervous sip from her empty glass.

"Why are you here again?"

"It's just me, Mrs. Corrigan. Jules. Remember me? There's nothing going on," Jules repeated.

"But that's just it! It's not just you, is it? Who's the other kid? I keep seeing this other kid. I'll get him, and then they'll believe me."

Katherine turned and crept back down the hall, muttering to herself and darting suspicious glances back at him. Cynthia was taking it all in and nodding like she was on the case as well and it was only a matter of time before the truth was revealed.

Jules moved over toward the stairs trying to make it look like he wasn't desperate to get away.

"I'll just go up and check on my homework with Gen, Mrs. Corrigan."

"Homework! What are they teaching you? There's something at that school . . ." She retreated into the dining room as Jules headed up the stairs.

He paused outside Gen's door. He could hear excited voices coming from within. The earlier feelings of intense jealousy started to simmer.

He knocked quickly and loudly and called out, "It's OK, it's me."

Genevieve flung open the door and Jules looked at her in amazement. She was wearing The Coat.

"Watch this! Bolero!" she cried.

And The Coat, which at this stage was actually a full-length cape, the kind of thing you would have worn riding a horse through a Russian winter in about 1780, pulled its hem in to above her waist, puffed out a little at the shoulders, grew a couple of tight sleeves and embroidered itself along the yoke to become a very classic jacket in the Spanish bolero style.

"Black and red, por favor!" Gen ordered.

The Coat turned black with dramatic red stitching.

"Not bad, eh? It has seven thousand styles already programmed, plus you can tell it to do anything else you want. And you can get the shoes to match!"

Gen was radiant with excitement, dancing around the room wearing Theodore's Coat and shoes. Theodore was sitting on Gen's bed clapping his hands and humming a flamenco tune. The JumpMan and remote were next to him and a panel on the front of the JumpMan was just closing up.

"Coat, how am I?" Gen yelled.

"Body temperature rising due to excessive exercise. Will need to take on fluids soon," reported The Coat. "You should try the latest GeneJuice. First juice made from the first fruit to be entirely genetically modified. No real fruits were harmed in the making of this juice. Gives you the energy you need—"

"Shut up, Coat!" Theodore and Gen yelled together, and Theodore got up laughing from the bed and started dancing with her.

Jules sat quietly on Gen's bed. He desperately wanted to have a turn at The Coat as well, but he didn't want to show it. He was insanely jealous of Gen getting to wear it and the simmering jealousy he kept feeling whenever he saw Gen and Theodore getting on like this, boiled over.

"Your mother's gone mad. She knows there's something going on," he said, trying to put a big dampener on everything.

"She's always mad! Long as she stops picking on me," said Gen. "Party dress!"

"Gen, this is serious. I think Cynthia knows everything too."

"Cynthia! Cynthia dobs on people when they pick their nose. Mum and Dad don't listen to her. Oh, a much brighter red than that, thank you!"

Jules could see nothing was getting through to the pair in front of him. They were now dancing like the grooviest party couple ever and Gen was wearing a tight-fitting, strapless, short dress that was so red it hurt to look at it.

Jules picked up the JumpMan remote.

"Put it down, Jules," Theodore ordered. "I think it's fixed. I'm going to do a test Jump in a minute, and then maybe I can go home."

Jules ignored him and continued studying the remote and reading the screen. There were two buttons with arrows on them, like a TV remote, and he flicked one of them a couple of times.

"I won't do anything stupid."

Jules hated the way Theodore treated him like he was some sort of under-evolved squid. Gen had gone on a Jump with him. Gen was getting to wear The Coat and the shoes. Jules's jealousy prowled around his stomach like an angry panther.

"Woosh, or wow as you would say." Theodore was delighted. "I didn't know The Coat would do this."

"You've never asked me," said The Coat.

Gen was circling the room and the party dress was now shimmering gold with red and pink flashes running through it. It was stunning.

"Genevieve, you look wonderful," said Theodore, rejoining her in the dance.

"What happens if I press this?" asked Jules.

"Just put it down, will you?" snapped Theodore. "If you

must play with it, like a little boy, then press the Games button on the bottom. Start at zongoid level and see how you go."

Jules seethed. He was humiliated beyond anything he'd ever experienced, and he was quite experienced in being humiliated.

"You're so smart, aren't you? Well, if you're so smart, why don't you just go back to where you came from? But you can't, can you? 'Cause this thing's broken. I bet if I pressed this big button here nothing would happen."

"Jules! Don't!" yelled Theodore. "Put the remote down!"

Theodore and Gen danced over to the bed and Theodore tried to wrestle the remote off Jules while Gen, who hadn't really noticed that anything was getting up Jules's nose, tried to keep on dancing with Theodore.

"Jules, don't," mimicked Jules. "Well, if she gets to wear The Coat, I want to have a Jump."

And he pointed the remote at the sphere and pressed the Go button.

They weren't in Gen's bedroom anymore.

They weren't in her house.

They weren't in her street.

The entire city had gone.

Jules suddenly felt cold and wet. The three of them were rolling over one another down a muddy slope. They stopped rolling when they bumped into a small bush that let loose a deluge of water over them. There were bushes and trees all around them.

"You Jumped us!" shrieked Gen.

"Quiet!" ordered Theodore, pointing through a gap in the trees.

Jules and Gen went still. In a clearing on the other side of the small gully, they could see about twenty or so human-looking creatures. There was a shallow cave in the hillside and two or three rudimentary-looking shelters made out of leaves and bark. The figures were short and very hairy. Some sat in small groups of three or four, a couple nursed babies, and a few children ran about playing with bits of fur. Two of the larger ones seemed to be on lookout and were staring back at them.

"Don't move," whispered Theo.

One of the lookouts stood up, scanning the hillside where they were hiding. He sniffed the air and then resumed his crouching position, looking all around but returning his scrutiny to their position every few seconds.

"Homo erectus," whispered Theodore. "Us, about a million years ago. Sort of half-ape, half-man."

~ Whoa, said Jules's brain. This thing really works.

Jules didn't move a muscle. Was he really back in time looking at cavemen?

"Thanks to the tiny brain of Jules, which seems to be about the same size as our ape-men ancestors over the way, we are now at a JumpSite called The First Word," said Theodore. "Want to stay and watch the fun?"

"Fun?" whispered Gen.

"It's hilarious. Keep your eye on the guy who's picking up the two bones."

"Shouldn't we go?" suggested Jules.

"Oh, so you wanted a Jump and now you don't? Could you make up your mind before you take these kinds of risks, next time?" said Theodore.

Jules turned his attention to the guy picking up the bones.

Like the others, he was hairy all over, but it was a light covering of hair, not furry like a monkey. His skin showed through the orangy-brown hair. He was filthy, with bits of mud matted in his hair, dirt embedded in the folds and cracks of his body, and caked under his thick fingernails. He didn't look very human, but his actions were unmistakable.

He gestured and squawked a bit to get the others' attention. He stuck the two bones in either side of his mouth, put one arm behind his back, and swung the other in front of him. He moved across the clearing with a slow lumbering gait, stopped and pointed at himself, and said, "Og."

A couple of the others glanced up. One of them did a kind of laughing thing, although it sounded more like someone choking and the look on his face was more threatening than cheerful, but most of the group paid no attention to the one lumbering about with the bones in his mouth.

"There it is," said Theodore. "You just heard the first word ever spoken."

"Og?" whispered Jules.

"What, did you think he'd say 'mammoth'?"

Jules looked back to where the speaker was lumbering up and down the clearing. He stopped and said "Og" again. He lumbered up to individuals, patted himself on his chest, and said, "Og." He jumped up and down in front of them and said, "Og, Og, Og, OG!"

Then the speaker turned away with a look of disgust and wandered back over to his side of the clearing. He took the bones out of his mouth and then threw them in the dirt. He sat on his bum, slumped forward, and thumped the ground, making angry grunting noises.

"I think he's trying to come up with the word for 'idiots,'" said Theodore.

The speaker sat up, shook his head, and picked up his bones. He tapped them together and seemed to be thinking. All at once he jumped up with a hopeful look on his face. He lumbered forward once more, only this time he raised the hand that was doing an impression of a trunk and made a trumpeting noise.

They all looked up at that. He stopped when he had their attention and once more said, "Og." The rest of the group looked at one another and then went back to picking lice out of each other's hair, or snoozing, or arranging rocks, or whatever they'd been doing. Everyone except for one of the younger ones. He, or she, it was hard to tell, came over and squatted in front of the one doing the mammoth impression.

"He's been doing this for about three weeks now," whispered Theodore. "He keeps on doing his mammoth impression and saying 'og.' The others just don't get it."

Jules was completely absorbed. It was such an amazing feeling, beyond any kind of excitement he'd ever known. He could believe what he was seeing, he just couldn't quite believe that he was here to see it.

"So these things are really us?"

"Evolution, my dear Jules," said Theodore kindly but patronizingly. "Get a few adventurous apes to come down from the trees and do better than the rest of the gang, and they get to reproduce. They start to stay down from the trees and the ones that are better adapted to that kind of living survive.

"There's more food, and they start to hunt other animals. Get more protein in your diet and you've got more time to sit around and think. Og Man's got so much time on his dirty little hands that he's dreamed up this wild idea of naming things. But it's hard to get that idea across when no one has ever named anything before."

"Look at the little kid," said Gen.

The young one who'd come over to squat with Og Man had found a couple of twigs in the dirt and stuck them in its mouth. It was now following Og Man around and doing a pretty good mammoth impression too. Og Man turned around and found he had a partner. The child immediately stopped doing it, except Og Man made some encouraging grunts and gestures and got the child to start again.

"Og," he said, pointing at himself and then at the child. "Og."

The child looked at him for a while, made a noise a bit like a chuckle, and then said, "Og."

Og Man squealed with delight. "Hgrgrrrrrrr!" he said. "Og! Og Og Og Og!"

The child jumped back, squealed as well, and then

lowered its head and charged at Og Man. "Og!" it said, taking a few steps back and looking at Og Man for approval.

"Og," said Og Man, reaching out and poking the child in the chest.

The child jumped and threw the bones in the air and then ran around to get one of the other young ones, yelling "Og!" as it went.

Og Man seemed to frown a little at this.

"It's tough when you're the only one doing the talking," commented Theodore.

"But the little one understands him," said Gen.

"Sort of," said Theodore. "The kid hasn't actually seen a mammoth. He thinks it's the name of the game. In about six months they find a dead mammoth, and Og Man takes the kid to see it. Then they start talking about the same thing. Give 'em a couple more generations and the descendants of this group can organize an Og hunt, and is that a wild thing to see."

"Can we go see it?" asked Jules eagerly.

"Oh, I thought you wanted to go home?" said Theodore. "It's pretty long and slow and three of them get stomped on in the process, so I don't know, maybe that's enough for a first Jump."

"Second," corrected Gen a little smugly.

"Yip, well, whatever. I think we probably should just

Jump back. We got away with this one, I'm going to have to go test this thing again—"

"Oh, please, just one more?" pleaded Gen, lowering her eyes and looking very appealingly at Theodore.

"Oh, OK. It's a pretty safe one. I mean, you may as well complete your introduction to the achievements of primitive man. Everyone in a huddle and holding hands. That's when we started talking. Want to see the Making of Fire?"

They held hands, closed their eyes, and Theodore pushed the big red button on the remote.

Jules and Gen opened their eyes. They were standing on gently rolling land at the base of very steep mountains. The ground was covered in tufts of grass and the occasional stumpy tree. Like the last Jump, they were looking over at a camp, this one slightly bigger with maybe thirty or so cavemen. The cavemen were bigger and looked distinctly human.

"Where are we?" asked Gen.

"When are we?" asked Jules.

"This is the Making of Fire JumpSite. I've been doing a project on this for school. All Time, it's 5:24 PM on 4 April, Fourteen Billion, Nine Hundred and Ninety-nine Million,

Nine Hundred and Twenty-four Thousand, Four Hundred and Fifty-seven ABB."

"ABB?"

"After Big Bang."

Gen and Jules looked over at the camp. This one looked like it had been there for a while.

"Are they people?" asked Gen.

"Nip, not really. We're people. Homo sapien. They're Neanderthals. They're like a kind of people who didn't survive. They did some good things, though. They did figure out how to make fire. Keep your eye on Sparky."

"Sparky?"

"Sparky the Wonder Neanderthal is his full title."

"So he's really smart?"

"Nip. He's a total twunt. He's been rubbing sticks together for about three months now. He's not trying to release the inert energy of the stick through friction, he's just mad and likes rubbing sticks together. He banged rocks together for two years before he became keen on sticks."

"Umm, Theodore. We're not invisible, are we?"

Theodore looked at Jules and then looked at where he was pointing.

The Neanderthals appeared a little upset. They were picking up long sticks and old bones and beating the ground with them. The smaller ones gathered up the two or three children and babies who'd been playing together and were retreating to the cave. The larger ones began beating their chests and snarling and pointing in the direction of Jules, Genevieve, and Theodore.

"Ahh, right. I'd forgotten about that."

The biggest Neanderthals formed themselves into a tight group of about twelve. The rest stood around what Jules assumed were the women and children and formed a guard. The ferocious group started moving in their direction.

"Umm, Theodore, isn't this when you'd use your jump off thing or whatever it's called?" asked Jules.

"JumpOut," corrected Theodore.

"Yeah. Didn't you say if you land in a lava flow or something you can jump on? Can we do it for an attack of the angry Neanderthals?"

"Not working."

"Huh?"

"Can't do a JumpOut while it's in Test Mode. It's reviewing itself. It's going to take a few minutes."

"Well, should we do something else?"

"Possibly not."

"Not? We should not do something? We just let these things come over here with the bones and the sticks?" Gen was sounding a little apprehensive.

"Well, we have to be very careful not to interrupt the Making of Fire."

"Can't Sparky make it tomorrow?"

"Who knows? The TimeJumping Code, remember? Don't Touch Anything. We're always invisible. We just watch. And it's never been part of the Making of Fire JumpSite that three of us turn up visible an hour before the discovery and get chased by the Neanderthal army. Oh my helix! Get out of here! Head for the end of the cliff!" Theodore was screaming as the crack unit of the Neanderthal army headed their way.

They turned and ran. Jules looked back over his shoulder. The Neanderthals weren't really as thick as their eyebrows, he observed. They'd broken up into three groups of four with two groups heading out to either side and one group coming straight after them.

Jules ran faster. Gen was right behind him, but Theodore was getting nowhere. He was running like, well, someone who doesn't really know how to run, thought Jules.

"Gen!" Jules yelled to Gen. "Head up to the top of the cliff. Find somewhere to hide. Use The Coat. Hide under it. Camouflage." He hoped that made sense and then he dropped back to pick up Theodore who was flopping along like an old seal. The Neanderthal commandos were gaining on them and were circling and sniffing them warily.

"You can't run, can you?" Jules panted.

"Not something we do, I'm afraid."

"OK, head for those bushes and I'll try to distract them."

"Don't forget about the JumpMan."

Theodore threw him the remote, and Jules looked back to where the JumpMan was sitting in the dirt, glinting in the last rays of sunshine. Great. In their panic, they'd taken off and left it sitting on the ground.

Theodore ducked down into a small thicket of bushes and crawled away. Jules ran in a different direction and then turned and stopped.

"Hey. Over here!" he yelled, bending down and picking up some stones.

The Neanderthals stopped about ten yards away from him and waited for his move.

Jules growled.

They growled back.

He yelled, "Just go away, you great hairy no-brains."

The Neanderthals looked at one another and then screamed. Very loudly and very high pitched. It was very painful.

Jules put one of the stones in his right hand, took aim, and threw it at the Neanderthals.

The four Neanderthal commandos immediately picked up rocks and threw them straight at his head. All four rocks came whizzing in perfectly on target. OK, thought Jules, they're probably quite good at throwing rocks.

Jules ducked and ran. At least he'd distracted them from Theodore and Gen. The Neanderthals had joined together again and were now all just chasing him.

Great, he thought. And now they seemed faster than before.

Maybe they'd been a bit scared and maybe they'd been deciding how dangerous these new creatures really were. But now their wariness had gone. They weren't scared of Jules at all.

Jules didn't need to turn around to know how close they were getting. He could hear them.

They were right behind him and having no trouble keeping up with him. They were grunting to one another and Jules wondered what the discussion was. Should they beat his head in with a rock when they got him? Should they drag him back to the cave and string him up for a week or two to see what he does? Should they eat him?

He risked a look back over his shoulder.

Yes, he was being chased by a dozen Neanderthals. They had jutting jaws and foreheads like craggy rock faces. A ridge of eyebrow was above their large eyes, and their broad noses covered about half of their faces. They had hair as thick as rope down to the middle of their backs and they were wearing skins and tied-up bits of old animal. They were cavemen, all right, and they looked as fit and as strong as anything would that had to run down young gazelles for its living.

A vague plan formed in Jules's mind. In the fading light he looked down at the JumpMan remote. There was the big Go button and two others above it. Both had little arrows pointing in opposite directions above them.

He flicked up the screen. "Test Mode. 60 seconds to end," he read.

He started to circle back to the JumpSite and to where the JumpMan was still sitting in the dirt. The Neanderthals stayed close behind him and began to grunt more vigorously. Were they closing in for the kill?

Jules hoped he had enough left in him for a sprint and he took off. The Neanderthals were a bit surprised at this sudden burst of speed but a couple of them took off after him.

Jules skidded into the dust and put one hand on the JumpMan. The Neanderthals surrounded him and started their high-pitched screaming again. One of them held up a bone and stepped forward into the circle.

Jules looked at the screen. "Test Mode. 10 seconds to end."

He picked up the JumpMan and started screaming

as well. The Neanderthals stopped for a moment and then all of them began to close in on him.

Jules counted down out loud, still screaming. "Three! Two! One!"

He pointed the remote at the JumpMan. This better work, he thought, and pressed one of the buttons with the arrows on it.

All went quiet.

No Neanderthals.

The cave was there and the landscape looked pretty much the same, but the Neanderthals had gone. Or more accurately, he'd gone. Jules had done a JumpOut. He'd figured a press of one of these buttons would send him somewhere, and he was right.

Jules looked at the cliff and the cave and felt a brief moment of terror as he thought about how wrong he could be with all of this. How long should he wait here? How long would it take for the Neanderthals to get over their shock at his disappearance and disperse?

He gave them two minutes. He couldn't wait any longer. He had to go back and get the others. He looked at the remote.

~ What do you think, brain? Should I press the opposite button to the one I pressed? Should I press the big button? Should I press the same button?

It was a moment like you see in action movies, where the actor has to decide whether to cut the green wire or the red wire to defuse the bomb. Get it wrong and everyone's in trouble.

~ The opposite one, said his brain. No, hang on. The same one. No, maybe it's the big one in the middle. No, it'd be the opposite one. No—

~ Thanks, brain. Don't know what I'd do without you.

He pressed the opposite button with the small arrow and held his breath.

It worked. He was back.

The Neanderthal militia were walking back to their cave, grunting and scratching their heads. They were puzzled by the way the three intruders had disappeared, but at least they were gone.

The sun was setting and Jules was hidden in the shadows of the cliff. Keeping low to the ground, he made his way over to where he thought Theodore was hiding.

"Theodore," he called as loudly as he dared.

"Here. Down here." Theodore looked out from under a bush. "Sorry to leave you out there, but well, you did just fine. Did you do a JumpOut?"

"Yeah, I guess I did."

"Good thinking. So, it seems to be working all right. Where's Gen?"

Jules and Theodore looked around them.

"I told her to go and hide up on the cliff. She must still be up there."

They looked up at the cliff top and at the enormous Moon as it rose over it. The Neanderthals were also looking up at the Moon, and howling.

"This is a big night for them. They howl at the Moon for a while and then Sparky discovers fire," said Theodore.

"So they keep looking up, right where Genevieve is hiding?"

"Yip." Theodore looked worried.

"What happens when Sparky makes fire?"

"Brilliant!" Theodore grabbed him. "It's any moment now. We can go get her then."

Jules nodded, and they both cautiously poked their heads up over the bushes and fixed their attention on Sparky.

As Theodore had said, Sparky the Wonder Neanderthal was a mammoth or two short of a herd. Never one to join in with the others, who'd been really annoyed at his habit of banging rocks together from sunrise to sunset, he was now rubbing a pointy stick into a flat stick while the rest of the tribe ignored him and either howled at the Moon or did chores around the camp.

Sparky was so skinny he looked half-starved, but he didn't seem to care. He hadn't noticed the earlier chase and had remained squatting off to one side of the camp, incessantly twirling his stick.

Did he have a hint of what might happen? No, he didn't even know what day it was. Well, neither did any of the others, but at least they were starting to recognize that there were days and seasons, and form some memories of past events. Sparky woke up after each deep and untroubled sleep to a fresh dawn, a yellow fireball rising in the east that he thought he'd never seen before. After watching in wonderment for a few moments, Sparky would sift through the dust for a bone and a bit of rotting fruit and that would be his breakfast. He'd circle the camp, find his twirling stick, and begin his work again. Slowly at first as he figured out again how to do it, and then with ease and vigor as his muscles remembered for him.

Jules and Theodore watched him. Sparky had been rubbing his sticks together for about three months and this was the first time anything had happened. He stopped and peered down at the flat stick on the ground.

"This is it," said Theodore. "Get ready to go. Sparky's just noticed a tiny wisp of smoke. Doesn't know what it is."

The rest of the tribe were still baying at the Moon, which was rising silver and shiny above the cliff. Jules wondered how Genevieve was coping up there. He hoped she didn't think the Neanderthals were howling at her.

A few of them had started to dance, shuffling around in a circle and stopping at the same point to howl. Others sat in the dirt and rocked back and forth but all seemed involved in the rudimentary performance.

Sparky resumed his rubbing. A few minutes later, Jules could see the smoke.

Sparky stopped again.

The smoke stopped.

Sparky stuck his stick in the groove he'd made and went for it, double speed.

The smoke sprang up again quickly and Sparky grunted. He went faster and faster and then leapt up with a scream.

Flame had shot forth from the flat stick and his twirling stick was on fire as well. He immediately dropped it to the ground, where it set fire to a pile of dry leaves and bracken, and Sparky shuffled back in terror toward the tribe howling at the Moon.

Several of them caught sight of the sudden flickering

light coming from behind them and grunted, pointing and pulling at the others to get their attention.

Sparky went back over and picked up a burning branch. One of the bigger males who'd chased Jules earlier approached Sparky.

Sparky swung the burning branch around in front of him. The big Neanderthal jumped out of the way.

Jules thought that Sparky almost smiled but perhaps just his eyebrow lifted a little and caught some of the light from the first fire made by man.

Sparky swung the branch again and this time took a step forward as well. The other Neanderthals all retreated toward the cave.

"See why it's such a popular spot? Does Sparky discover fire and set down to roast himself a lizard? No, Sparky goes on the attack," said Theodore. "C'mon, they're all watching Sparky now."

Jules and Theodore scuttled away from their hiding place. They kept bent double to the ground as they ran because the Moon was lighting up the place like daytime.

They ran up the ridge to the top of the cliff. Below them, Sparky was yelling excitedly and setting fire to more grass and dead leaves. The tribe seemed unsure of what to do with him.

"Gen!" hissed Jules. "Gen! Where are you? Don't worry, it's us."

"Yeah, well I thought it was you. I don't think the cavemen know my name yet."

Gen rose up from near their feet. She'd been under The Coat.

"You got The Coat to blend in with the ground!" said Theodore. "How did you do that?"

"Took forever. I was ordering up Desert Sand, Baked Wheat Biscuit, Dusty Taupe—took me ages to get the color right. And I couldn't get it to shut up. I was thirsty so it just kept on trying to sell me drinks. I found the volume, though. Hey, Jules, I saw the whole thing. It was fantastic! How about that run you took them on and then when you just disappeared, I nearly lost it, I thought you'd just gone and left us—"

She was interrupted by a screech from below.

Sparky had noticed them up on the cliff. The three of them were standing up and were clearly silhouetted against the rising Moon. Sparky had raised his burning branch and was waving it back and forth at them. He was screeching something over and over, and now the others were turning to see what had caught his attention.

They all joined in on Sparky's screech.

Theodore looked down at them. "You know," he said. "The Timejumping Code is so right. Don't Touch Anything. I mean, we're not even touching anything, we're just standing here, but you know what I think they're thinking? We're

Moon gods. And we brought fire from the Moon to them. Each flame that flickers will remind them of us, and every full Moon, they'll go crazy hoping we'll return. I think we just started religion. Time to go."

Theodore took the remote. "Hold hands and put the other hand on the JumpMan. Let's hope this works."

Theodore dialed up Return on the remote and pressed the Go button. They vanished just as Sparky suddenly found himself becoming that highly desirable thing, a high priest. The first High Priest of the Moon Gods and the Firebringers, leading the rest of the tribe each full Moon in a ritual of chanting without which, Sparky tells them, the Moon gods will come and take the fire back.

They were back in Gen's big welcoming upstairs attic room. The room anyone over twelve and a half wants. Up in the roof where no one will bother you. Never had it looked better to any of them and they collapsed into a grateful hugging heap on Gen's bed. For about two seconds. Then they got embarrassed and stood up, shook themselves down, and found things to laugh about like the prehistoric dust on their clothes and the strange-smelling dung stuck to the bottom of Jules's shoes.

"Yip, well, for first-time TimeJumpers you did OK," Theodore grudgingly admitted. "You know, I feel really not well. I've got to lie down." And he fell back on Gen's bed, coughed a little, and put a hand over his eyes.

"You hungry, Theo? I'm starving," said Jules. His earlier jealousy had gone. They'd survived. And even though it was Jules who'd Jumped them out there in the first place, it was Jules who'd got them back.

"Nip. Nothing, thank you," replied Theodore. "I feel a bit weak, kind of achy in the joints."

"You'll be all right."

And then they noticed Cynthia.

She was sitting up the other end of the long room, a big grin all over her face, looking like she was about to burst.

"I knew it! I knew it! You two came up here ages ago and I came up and you weren't here and I knew you'd have to come back! I knew there was something going on, but I didn't think of anything like this! You just appeared. How did you do that? Where have you been? Who's the other kid? Does his hair always do that?"

The Coat decided to speak up as well.

"Volume Override for Medical Emergency. Large amounts of gooey liquid appear to be forming in your nostrils, Theo. You feel tired, dry in the throat, and snuffly. Slight temperature. Condition unknown. Oh, and by the way, your total number of TimeCode breaches now means you'll lose your Jumping Licence pretty much forever. Setting yourself up as a religion or a god is strictly forbidden, as is the bringing back of unidentified dung. Of course, a JumpMan's not the only way a kid can look cool this summer. Surf the wind with the Kite that'll carry you to heights you've only dreamt of—"

"Shut up, Coat," said Theodore. "You know this imp?" he asked Gen.

"She's my sister. Cynthia, meet Theodore. Theodore, Cynthia."

"Hi. So what's the trick?" asked Cynthia. "Can I have a go?"

Gen knew she had a tough one ahead of her. Her little sister could not be allowed to leave this room with the information she had. She would either have to wipe Cynthia's mind clean, kill her, or find some way of buying her silence. She looked around the room for an effective bribe.

Not much there. Cynthia already had all her old dolls and stuff, and she'd already got Gen's old room. What would she want?

Gen looked down at her dusty clothes and then across at Cynthia. Gen smiled.

"Hey, Cynth. Watch this."

Cynth watched her.

"Coat! Barbie dress," ordered Gen. The Coat turned into

a pink Barbie dress that Barbie would have killed Ken for.

"Tutu. White," she ordered again. Again The Coat obliged with a perfect tutu that any dying swan would have killed another dying swan for.

"Snow White." The Coat became the perfect Snow White dress that the wicked queen would have killed her for if she wasn't already poisoning her with the apple for being the fairest in the land.

Cynthia assumed the standard gobsmacked expression and her entire being was consumed with desire. Want it, she drooled. Friends will envy me. All will envy me. I will be the queen of Year Three and there will be no defying me. I will decide who wears The Coat and who doesn't. Powerrrr.

"Do you want a go?" Gen inquired sweetly.

Cynthia looked at her like she was mad. There are people around who wouldn't want a go?

"Well, you can have a go now and if you don't say anything to anyone, not Mum, not Dad, not anyone ever, you can take it to school on Friday."

"Hang on," said Theodore. "She can't—"

"Be quiet, Theodore. This is family. Never get between sisters doing deals on clothes."

Gen had Cynthia mesmerized. Cynthia wanted The Coat. She felt the awesome power of The Coat and knew what it could do for her. She would have The Coat and she promised that she would tear her tongue out with tweezers before she would tell anything of what she knew.

"OK. You can have a little go now, but don't forget! Say anything, and you will never see The Coat again!" Gen resisted the urge to do a wicked witch laugh but she was very tempted.

Jules was feeling tired, hungry, and in need of a shower. He caught sight of the clock on Gen's desk. It was eleven o'clock. Oh no, he thought. His dad, the little talk. He had to go.

"I better go," he said. "Look, I'll see you in the morning, right? Try for a Jump home then, eh Theo?"

But Theodore just feebly raised his hand from his head, waved limply at Jules, and sneezed. Jules ran out the door, a little worried about Theodore's health but more worried about what his dad was going to do when he got home.

He ran down the stairs with Cynthia dancing behind him, chanting in her horrible singsong manner: "I'm going to get a Barbie dress that's better than anyone else's, I'm going to get a Barbie dress that's better—"

"Cynthia!" snapped Jules.

"What?"

"I think the idea was, you get a go of The Coat if you shut up about everything until Friday. OK?"

"Oh what, and are you going to stay here and watch me every single second of every single hour of every single day until then and make sure I don't say one single word and then go and dob on me?"

~ *Can we get away from that please? requested his brain.*

~ *My thoughts exactly, replied Jules as he took the rest of the stairs two at a time. Never argue with a seven-year-old in full brat mode. He was sure Cynthia would end up giving them away, but there was nothing he could do about it.*

He felt exhausted. Was this still the same day that they'd found Gen's mothers in the headmaster's office? He still had homework to do. There was probably some sort of test tomorrow or something due.

He felt stiff and sore from running away from Neanderthals. How far had he run? Up and down that dusty plain, back to get the JumpMan, up the cliff to get Gen. He needed to go to bed.

Something like a hen's foot latched onto his forearm and wouldn't let go. He turned around and there was Gen's mum, as mad as before.

"Back now, are we? Everyone back, tucked up in beddy-byes?" Her voice was brittle and grating like a wicked stepmother in a bad pantomime.

"Not there before, were we? No one there when I peeked in. Or were you all there? I can't tell anymore. Are you here now?" And she tightened her grip on his forearm and peered into his eyes.

The doorbell rang.

"Who's that? More of you? Sending messages through the doorbell? Ding dong ding ding ding dong dong dong." She dragged him over to the door and flung it open.

Jules's dad was standing there.

"Katherine," he said. "Jules. What's going on?"

"Daddy's here!" Katherine started singing, "He comes, he goes, and no one knows, but Daddy's come to count his toes!" She danced back up the hallway leaving Jules and his dad standing at the door.

"I gave you an hour," said his dad in a strained voice. "And then I let you have a half-hour more. It's eleven o'clock!"

Jules had been so busy travelling in time he'd forgotten the time.

"What have you been doing? I thought we understood each other when you left. Nine-thirty you were going to be home. Don't worry, you said, I won't be late. Mate, I didn't want to bust in here and cause a scene but by eleven o'clock, I'm getting pretty worried."

Tony strode off down the footpath with Jules scurrying along behind him.

"What am I going to do with you?" Jules's dad was muttering to himself as Jules caught up to him. He stared at Jules for a moment and shook his head, then they walked the last few blocks home in silence.

When they were inside their house, Tony said, "Go on, just go up to bed. We'll talk about this in the morning."

"Umm, Dad?"

"What now?"

"I'm actually really hungry. Can I just have some toast or something?"

Tony looked down at his son and his face softened a little bit.

"C'mon then. I need a cup of tea myself."

They headed into the kitchen and Jules could feel that his dad wanted to say something. He watched Jules making toast, sitting there patting his hands together in front of his lips in awkward silence except for when he said things like, "There you are then," and "OK, toast and tea."

Jules was finishing his sixth piece of toast and wondering if he should have a bowl of cereal as well when finally Tony got started.

"Jules," he said.

"Yes, Dad?"

"I've been speaking to your mother."

His mother?

"I think we should all get together and talk about a few things. Family meeting, mate."

Jules decided he'd need the cereal to get through this. The last family meeting had been when his mother left.

That had been about what Jules was and wasn't allowed to do then. Sounded like more of the same.

"She's going to come down and we'll have dinner together on Friday night."

Friday night? Jules turned around from the cereal cupboard.

"Umm, does it have to be Friday night?" he asked.

"What? You have other plans?"

"Well, no. Yes. Sort of." Jules fumbled around. He still had faint hopes that he was going to the movies with Gen.

~ *Pretty faint, said his brain. You haven't even asked her yet.*

~ *Yes I did, she just got distracted.*

Out loud he said, "Well, there's a few of us thinking of going to see *My Hamburger is an Alien* on Friday night."

"Who?" asked Tony.

"Oh, you know, Max and maybe, umm, Gen."

His dad pushed his chair back.

"You and Gen. You're going out with her, right?"

"No, I'm not, Dad. Really. It's not like that, Dad." Jules squirmed. This was awful.

"Look, mate. We need to talk about this stuff. I want your mother involved as well. She can only do this Friday. That's it. Don't start arguing about it, you're in enough trouble right now."

Jules looked away, wishing he was back running away

from cavemen. It had all seemed so simple then.

"Mate, do I have to spell it out? It's pretty obvious that stuff with you and girls and going out is happening already, and you and your mother and me need to decide what the ground rules are. OK?"

Tony was standing up now, and the finger was pointing at Jules. The law had been laid down. Jules felt his mood plummet. A few hours ago everything had been great.

"Don't push it, OK? We'll talk about it on Friday and we'll sort everything out then." Tony took his mug over to the sink. "Now, come on, finish that up and off to bed."

Jules dragged himself up to his room. Great. It didn't matter if Gen had heard the invitation, if he got to ask her out again, or anything anymore. He wasn't going out. He'd lost. Theodore had won. Theodore would wake up in the morning feeling fine and they'd spend the day going to watch gladiator fights or the continents split or something and he couldn't even suggest they go to a movie. Oooh, and what about Max? What would he rather tell Max, that Gen had said no, or that his dad wouldn't let him go out? Fantastic. It just kept getting better.

~ Hey, said his brain. Could you stop all this? I really need some rest. Who knows what we're going to have to face tomorrow?

~ That's exactly the problem, said Jules.

Meanwhile . . .

QUINCY CARTER BARELY LOOKED UP WHEN SOLLY BOOLOO SHMUFFLED INTO HIS OFFICE. Many people had tried to find a word to describe the movements of Solly. He was very large, and underneath the layers of fat you could see the muscles, and the tone that had once been there. He always moved at whatever pace suited him. He came into the room with a lazy authority, and his walk was something between a shuffle and a march. A schmuffle.

He and Quincy went back a long way. Solly had started the Code Cops and was still in charge. He didn't knock when he came into Quincy's office.

He'd been at the side of the stage when Theodore had disappeared and since then had been organizing the search.

"You want the latest?" he asked Quincy.

"I want more than the latest," said Quincy, rising from the couch.

"Been an interesting day. Want to know who we found?"

"If it's not the kid, I don't want to know."

"Oh, you want to know. Have a look."

Solly pointed to the screen and up came pictures of Franklin Nixon jumping about trying to get everyone's attention.

"Franklin! How did you find him?"

Solly shrugged. "Got a report from Site Monitoring that someone had been yelling in Speakish at the Great Pyramid. Went and had a look and found Franklin chasing some kids about."

"Kids?"

"Yip. And you're going to want to see this too."

Solly forwarded the images on the screen. He stopped and zoomed in on one of the kids being chased by Franklin.

"That's the kid! The winner! Theodore. You got him!"

"Yip, ahh, you're not going to like this. We got Franklin, and we've brought him back. But we missed the kid."

Quincy looked at Solly and Solly recoiled slightly. There was a look of utter contempt in Quincy's eyes that in all their years of working together, Solly had never seen. He nodded slowly. He was starting to suspect that there was more to this than just a lost kid, and some public relations damage. What it might be, Solly didn't want to know. He continued with his report.

"But then we found them again."

"Them?"

"He's not alone. At the pyramid he was with a girl. Now there's a boy as well and they've been to the First World and the Making of Fire."

Quincy tried to contain his seething impatience.

"You haven't got him, have you?"

"Sorry. Nip."

Quincy turned around. He wanted very much to break something, to scream some more, and have a full-on tantrum like he hadn't had since he was four and a half.

"Solly." Quincy's voice had an edge that would have sliced steel. "Solly, I really don't care if you get a report of them setting fire to the Colosseum. Next time you slob in here, you'd better have Theodore Pine with you. Otherwise, don't come in. Oak eye?"

"Oak eye," agreed Solly. "You'd want me to tell you that someone did a Rewind in early Mil 3 though, wouldn't you?"

Solly had a slight smile on his face as he held out a report from Duncan Noong.

Quincy turned.

"Well. Are you going to stand here, or would you like to go and start tracking my missing JumpMan?"

chapter six

Running Out of Time

Jules had been asleep about thirty seconds when he heard tapping on the window. He looked at the clock. It was 5:30 AM. So it was longer than thirty seconds, but it didn't feel like it.

What was that noise? The tapping came again, harder this time and he heard a voice calling softly, "Jules! Jules!"

It was Gen. He threw the doona back and hobbled over

to the window. The sun hit him painfully in the eye as he pulled back the blind. Gen was standing outside, one hand raised to tap again.

"You've got to come over. Theodore's really sick."

"You want me to come over now? Do you know how much trouble I'm in already? Dad'll kill me if he catches me."

"You've got to come over! Just come and see. You can get back here before he gets up."

He had to go. If he didn't, Gen would never talk to him again. But if he went and got caught, his life was over. Jules couldn't remember a time when he'd had to make so many decisions. And it was never like choosing between two good things. Or even one good thing and one bad thing so that the choice was easy. It was always between two things just as bad as each other. And whatever he chose to do, it would end up in trouble.

Jules threw on some clothes. He slid the window up and stepped out.

"What's happened?" he asked as they walked quickly through the sunrise toward Gen's place.

"He's coughing and wheezing, complaining about a sore throat. Sneezes a lot," said Gen.

Jules stopped.

"Hang on. Am I risking all this because Theodore has a *cold*?"

"Not just a cold. Bits of him are disappearing and then reappearing around the room."

"What?"

"Well, you'll see. At the moment, it's just a finger or two. Sometimes his nose, but he says it's going to get worse. They disappear for a second and then reappear on the sofa or on my desk or sometimes we can't find them at all, until they come back again."

They let themselves in the front door and went upstairs.

Theodore was lying on Gen's bed. The Coat had turned itself into a neatly patterned, thick quilt. In between dispensing information, it would say "There, there" in a very comforting way.

"Body temperature, a little above normal, nothing to be alarmed about," The Coat reported. "There, there. Mucus expulsion rate very high. Runny eyes, headache, all over terrible. Can I recommend Dr. Noddy's Hot-tot Toddy? Teddy got noddy head that wants to be a-beddy bed?"

"Shut up, Coat." Gen sighed. "Does he look like a three-year-old to you?"

Gen and The Coat were old friends now.

Theodore seemed reasonably complete when Jules first saw him. But as he got closer to the bed, he noticed that beside him on the pillow was a big toe. Jules assumed it was Theodore's. As he looked at the toe in horror, it disappeared, hopefully reattaching itself to Theodore's foot.

Theodore looked terrible. His hair was a mournful yellow, blipping on and off with all the zip of a bored lighthouse.

"What'll we do?" asked Jules.

"I've no idea," said Gen. "I had to come and get you. He says the JumpMan's pretty ready to go, but he won't Jump while he's sick. Something about wiping everyone out."

"With a cold?"

"He thinks it's worse than that."

"Well, let's explain and then get him to Jump."

"And what if he leaves his toes behind?"

Jules had to concede that might be a problem, but he couldn't hang about now. If his dad caught him out this morning, after last night, they'd be having little talks every night for a month and he'd never be allowed out again.

"Can you look after him till after school?"

"I suppose so. I'll tell Mum I'm sick and then just stay up here."

"Cynthia? Will she blab?"

"I can handle Cynthia. I've still got The Coat."

Theodore stirred, coughed, and then looked over at them.

"Hi. I'm dying," he said.

"Don't say that," said Gen. Jules felt a stab of jealousy as he usually did whenever Gen was nice to Theodore. It was awful. After yesterday and all its drama, he now liked Theodore. But he wished Gen didn't seem to be quite so concerned and close to him. And how long was he going to be here? What if he never went back?

~ Oh, you're a really nice guy, said his brain.

~ You make me think this stuff, retorted Jules.

~ Do not.

~ Do so.

~ Look, I might be the same age as you, said his brain, but I'm not going to go on with this childish little tussle.

Theodore was struggling to sit up. He looked around for a tissue. He carefully selected one and then blew his nose extremely loudly for about a minute and a half.

"Look at this stuff," he said, offering the contents of the tissue for their inspection.

"Thank you, Theodore. I'm pretty familiar with snot," said Jules.

"But he's not," said Gen.

"Not what?" asked Jules.

"Familiar with snot."

"Really?"

"Really," said Gen. "I had to teach him to blow his nose."

Jules looked from one to the other trying to imagine what that must have been like. Couldn't have been pleasant and he felt pleased about that.

"We don't get colds. Never heard of them," said Theodore.

"Listen," said Gen, leaning forward. "I'm sorry to bring this up, but your toes are under my desk. What's going on?"

Theodore stopped exploring his nose.

"Particle dropout," he said in a hoarse whisper. "Oh, nip. I'm getting particle dropout."

"What's particle dropout?" Gen asked.

"It used to happen with some of the early machines. When people Jumped Present. Mostly when they went for too long. Go for a day or more and they could start to lose bits. They would JumpBack and at that precise moment something fizzled out and was left behind. You see a few old TimeJumpers without a foot or an earlobe or something. And there's the famous case of the Halfman who managed to live for three years without his entire right side."

Theodore slumped back on the pillow, sniffling.

Gen looked desperately at Jules.

~ Can't let her down now. You've got to do something.

~ Do something? What? Cure the common cold? Put his body back together? Dad's probably up by now and I'm grounded forever.

Jules shrugged helplessly. "We're going to have to tell someone," he said.

"We can't, Jules," said Gen.

"Don't tell anyone!" rasped Theodore. "Better I stay here and never go back than you do that." He collapsed again, exhausted from talking.

"You're going to have to JumpBack then, Theo!" said Jules.

"I can't. Go back with this, I could wipe everyone out." Theo spoke in a strained whisper and then his eyes closed and he appeared to go to sleep.

"Jules! What are we going to do?"

Jules felt like he was being offered a choice between various ways of amputating his own head. He had no idea what to do. He felt helpless and he had to go.

"Gen, I'm sorry. I'll come back after school. I'll think of something."

As he rushed to the door, he saw Gen's face crumple into tears. Great, he thought. Nothing I can do, but I have managed to make her cry. Perfect.

He bolted down the stairs and ran back home. He snuck in the front door and back into his bed about two minutes before his dad came in to wake him up.

As soon as he walked into school, Jules was pounced on by three-quarters of the four-headed monster.

"Where's Gen?" asked Sonja.

"She's sick," answered Jules.

"Where's Theo?" asked Kyeela.

"Umm, gone home," answered Jules.

"Is Gen going out with you or with him?" asked Bonnie, cutting to the chase.

"I don't know," answered Jules, pushing through them and ignoring the cries of "Ooooo, he said 'I don't know.' Bet that means she's going out with him!"

Jules plunged farther into the mass of unfamiliar faces, swinging schoolbags, and all the hectic chaos of a few minutes before the first class of the day. Max was waiting by his locker.

"Hi, Julie," said Max.

Great. Now he was going to be called Julie.

"So," Max continued. "Are we on for Friday night? Didja ask her out?"

"Yeah, I did. Well, no. I didn't," said Jules. "I mean, I did, but something happened."

"Well? What did she say?" asked Max.

"She didn't say no."

"Did she say yes?"

"No."

"What did she say?"

"She got distracted."

Max looked unimpressed. "You couldn't have asked her right."

"What do you mean?"

"Well, if you ask it right, they're never distracted." Max was full of this kind of worldly advice. He had four brothers, all older, and he was always spouting this kind of stuff as though he had heaps of experience with girls. The only thing he had lots of experience in was eavesdropping on his brothers.

"Did you say, 'Oh, baby, you're so beautiful, you've just got to come with me and Max this Friday night and make sure you bring that fox Sonja along as well'?"

"Shut up, Max. I'm not going to tell you what I said."

"I can't help you then," said Max. "You're on your own."

And Jules was left reflecting on how right Max was. He was on his own.

The day went from ordinary to extremely ordinary. Jules worried about Gen and Theodore all day. He was marked as absent because he didn't speak up in his home class when the roll was being marked and then was given detention for being late when he tried to explain that he'd been there all along. If he wasn't worried about the two of them alone together, he was worried about Theodore being sick. What should they do? Take him to a hospital? Call a doctor? Tell his dad? What would they say to Tony? "You're right, Dad. Gen and I aren't doing homework. And we're not doing that either," he would hasten to add. "We're looking after a boy from three thousand years in the future who got here with a thing called a JumpMan. Why, only last night, we used it to watch fire get made for the first time. But now the kid is sick and afraid to return to his own time. What should we do, Dad?"

That wouldn't work.

There was a test in Comparative Media. It wasn't hard. For example, the first question was:

Soap operas can be identified because

(a) Everyone sings all the time.

(b) There's lots of soap.

(c) All the ladies wear helmets with horns on them.

(d) They've been on TV for years and no one knows why.

Jules was so preoccupied he picked (c).

He sat in the wrong class for an entire period, oblivious of everyone's stares and whispers.

In Science, when the teacher asked, "Does anyone still believe that the world is flat?" up went his hand. And then, at the end of the class when he was meant to hand in a completed report on an experiment involving blue liquid and litmus paper, he handed in his lunch order.

In Math they began a whole new topic, algebra. He didn't hear a word the teacher said and never really understood algebra for the rest of his life.

At lunchtime he had to make do with a sausage roll and a bottle of pineapple juice because his Science teacher was giving his lunch order an F. He burnt his lips on the outside of the sausage roll and chipped a corner off a front tooth on the frozen middle bit. Still hungry and feeling sick after drinking pineapple juice with a half-cooked sausage roll, he slumped off to Life Class.

Life Class was considered by parents and teachers to be the most important two periods of the week. This was when the school taught everything that everyone else thought schools should be teaching these days. Nutrition, Personal Hygiene, the Dangers of HIV/AIDS, Drugs, Relationships, Multiculturalism, Basic Banking and Finance, Childrearing, Personal Identity, Self-esteem, Youth Suicide, Eating Disorders, and Civics. The students considered it a colossal bludge.

Jules slumped at his desk as an emergency teacher, who had no idea of what the class was meant to be doing, walked in. She wrote her name on the board.

"Hi, I'm Ms. Sikowski. Now, I don't know what to teach you today. No one left me any notes, and no one else seemed to know. So let's use this time to catch up on work, do some homework, or maybe just talk quietly among yourselves. If you keep the noise level down then I won't have to get heavy and we'll all get through this OK."

The class exploded into mayhem. A fight broke out in one corner. Students slapped on headphones, cranked up a mix they'd made themselves, and then talked loudly over the top of it. Six kids pulled out Gameboys and the bleeps and jaunty melodies punctuated the steady static of high-level conversation. Mobile phones called mobile phones on the other side of the room. Gossip was traded and plans laid. It was a party in room 274.

"That's not what I meant." Ms. Sikowski struggled to be heard. "C'mon, you're high school students now."

Jules looked around him, then picked up his books and bags and walked to the front of the room. This is a double period to the end of the day, maybe I can get out of here, he thought.

"Excuse me," he said.

Ms. Sikowski was chewing her nails and playing with her cigarette lighter.

"Stop that! You two, that's enough!" she shouted at no one in particular and with no conviction whatsoever.

"Excuse me, Ms.?"

Ms. Sikowski looked warily at Jules. Why was this boy standing in front of her? Was he about to let a cane toad go or something?

"Ms., I actually would like to do some homework? Is it OK if I go to the library?"

One less, thought Ms. Sikowski. Why not? She nodded, watching him leave.

As Jules closed the door, he heard six other boys yell out, "Miss, I want to study too. Can I go to the library, too please? Miss, you let him go, we'll go there, OK?"

He hurried off to the front gate before something happened to drag him back in.

When Jules came up into Gen's bedroom, she barely looked at him.

"Hi," he said, and she gave him a limp smile in return. Theodore lifted a bleary head from his pillow. He looked sick. And he was also crying.

"Theodore," asked Jules. "What's wrong?"

He gestured at the television. "Blaney wants to leave Sue-Ellen. How can he do that? Can't he see her heart's breaking? Sure she can't decide between him and Troy but she never lied to Blaney. She just needs time, Jules, time, that's all she needs and then she can decide. That slow lingering close-up on her face with the single tear running down her cheek. I've never seen anything so sad."

Jules looked at Gen. "What on Earth is he talking about?"

"He's been watching TV all afternoon."

"Oh, it's so wonderful," burst out Theodore. "How can you bear to turn it off?"

"Well, we've been watching it for a while," said Jules.

"Oh, sure, but the drama of it all! Those poor people. They cover their faces with makeup and make their hair so big and perfect to hide the pain of their lives. Don't you understand that? And they're so well dressed. Why don't you wear clothes like that?"

"You think I should wear clothes like the people on *The Bold and the Beautiful*?"

"You'd look great in a cream sports coat and some nice slacks. I can get The Coat to do it for you, if you like?"

"That's very kind, Theodore, but really, I'm happy with what I've got on." Jules looked at his T-shirt and baggy pants and worn-out trainers. Maybe he should spruce up a bit, but he wasn't about to try and look like someone on afternoon television.

"And then all those poor people on the next show. How did they find so many priests who want to be strippers?

And so many women who want to marry them?

"And then that wonderful program with the big fluffy bear who doesn't speak. Children must love that show. All those songs and that funny man with the propeller on his hat who tells you what the bear is saying. I sang all the songs. Lot of ads, though. Can't you afford one without ads?"

Jules saw what he meant.

"You mean like The Coat?"

Theodore nodded and then fell back on the pillow unconscious.

"He's been like this all afternoon," said Gen. "He needs some sleep. He hardly slept at all last night. If he doesn't sleep now, he's not going to get any better."

Jules went and looked at him. He wondered if Theodore was holding together any more than he had been this morning. He soon noticed that Theodore's left arm was now down on the floor and the fingers on his hand were tapping the carpet like they were impatient to get back to where they belonged.

Jules sat back and picked up the JumpMan remote. He had no idea what they should do. Gen and Theo were right. They couldn't tell anyone. There was something about the whole watching history and not interfering thing that just seemed right to Jules. They go and tell someone about him, and the worst thing that could happen is that someone might believe them. Then it'd be everywhere. He'd be all over the television in five minutes and then five minutes later he'd be on some show like the one Theodore had been watching: "Women Who Love TimeJumpers And Would Go To The End Of Time With Them." So they couldn't tell anyone. But they couldn't just let Theodore's particles spill about everywhere. At the moment they were just popping up around the room, but what if they began to roam a bit farther and ended up downstairs or out on the street? In fact, where was that left arm?

Jules found it behind the sofa.

He sat down and looked at the JumpMan, then he picked up the remote and began to flick through the pre-sets. As long as he didn't press the Go button, nothing could happen.

He looked down at the remote. The screen read, "Home."

He looked up at Gen. "I'm going Home," he announced.

Gen looked scathingly at him. Theodore's arm was back with him, but his thumb was flopping about on the pillow.

"Oh, OK, Jules. It was just great when you went off to school this morning, so yeah, why don't you go home. That's great," said Gen in a voice dripping with sarcasm. "I can handle everything here. You going to watch a video, maybe ring some friends?"

"No. I'm not going to my home. I'm going to go to his Home."

"Theodore's home?"

Jules held up the remote so Gen could read the screen.

"You're going to Jump?"

Jules nodded, although he wished he'd come up with some other idea entirely.

"You can't," Gen said. "It's too dangerous. What does Home mean anyhow?"

"It means Home. Look, there's nothing else on these pre-sets like it. I don't even know what these things are. But look, Home is just one word, everything else has dates and space–time coordinates. This one is just the word Home. We can tell them where Theodore is."

Gen walked around for a bit.

"How do we know it's going to work?"

"He was about to go himself. And it's not the JumpMan that's not working. It's him. He's sick. Look at him." Theodore was hard to look at at the moment as his right leg was over the other side of the room leaning up against the door. "There's no one here who can help us. The only help is in his time, at his Home."

Gen stopped walking and came over close to him.

"You'll do this?"

"I guess so."

"I better come too."

"No. Someone's got to stay here."

"Why?"

"To look after Theo. And what if, you know, umm . . ."

"What if you don't come back? Jules, you can't do this."

"Well, I think you've got about two minutes to think of something else, or I am going to have to do this."

Jules looked at the JumpMan. It was like having a bomb in the room, set to go off, and he had to pick it up, run outside, and toss it somewhere it wouldn't do any harm.

Gen was silent.

"It's up to us, Gen."

Gen felt very strange. Nothing had ever been up to her before.

"OK," she said. "I'll stay here. You Jump."

"OK."

It felt to both of them like they should say something very important, but neither had any idea how to say it. They held each other's gaze for a moment and then Jules picked up the JumpMan in one hand, and held the remote in the other. He checked the pre-set. It still read "Home." He closed his eyes and press the Go button.

When Jules opened his eyes he was standing in a darkened room. He could hear birdsong, and there was a breeze blowing through the room from behind him. A blind was pulled down over an open window and Jules could see a bed. He had the impression that it was a mild, warm kind of day outside.

Wow, Jules thought. I'm three thousand years in the future.

~ *You sure? How do you know you're not next door?*

~ *You ever seen a room like this? replied Jules.*

~ *True, said his brain.*

Jules had been in a lot of rooms belonging to people his own age and though each room might have its own individual features, they were all identical in one respect: they were always a mess. This room was completely empty. There was nothing in it at all. No books, no posters, no old skateboard, no clothes everywhere, no pile of magazines, no TV, no stereo, no anything.

Is this it? The "Home" on the JumpMan remote?

"Where is everything?" he said quietly to himself.

The walls answered him.

"For a full list of available clothing, reference material, games, and current entertainment, please say your password. Could you speak a little louder, please? Your last request was at my lowest threshold."

Jules leapt out of his skin. He looked around him, but there was no one there. He held his breath and tiptoed to the door.

"Password, please," the walls persisted. "Do you need your clothes? Would you like some decorations on the wall? I'm just downloading action shots of the Crab Nebula that are out of this world. Oh, I think I made a joke. My humor chip must be working again."

Jules opened the door and slipped out into a hallway. He guessed if The Coat could talk, then why not the walls as well. Must be hard to get a sense that you're ever alone if the nearest chair or T-shirt is programmed to start chatting away, Jules thought. Although, as he thought that, he realized that he'd never felt so completely alone as he did right now, standing in an empty hallway outside an empty bedroom belonging to a kid who was three thousand years away.

~ I'm here, his brain piped up.

I feel so much better, thought Jules.

The hallway was as bare as Theodore's room. No hall table, or chair, or bike, or paintings on the wall. Did everything slide back into the walls? If you wanted a hat rack, did you simply ask for one?

Everything was silent and still. There was no traffic noise, no car horns or buses grinding by. No radio on next door, no kids playing on swings in the backyard. Just the twittering of birds and the wind rustling the blinds. The house didn't feel large, but it felt very open. As though you could just peel the walls back and feel the mild breeze and look out all around.

Jules walked quietly along the hallway and looked into the rooms going off it.

All were empty. As he walked he became increasingly nervous. Where was he? Was this the right place? He didn't think the future would be quite so bare. Hang on, he could hear something. There was an incredibly loud thumping noise in his ears.

~ *It's your heart.*

~ *It's so loud.*

~ *That's what happens when you're terrified out of your brain. Not that you are. Because I'm still here.*

~ *Brain, why do you always make me feel better and worse at the same time?*

~ *I'm a brain. We do some amazing things. What about you? What are you going to do?*

Decision time again.

"Hello," he called out quietly.

"Hello," he repeated a little bit louder.

"There's no one here. Wherever here is," said Jules, almost crying.

"Well, *you're* here," said the walls.

Jules leapt again.

"Hello? Yes, I am here. Hello? Umm, who are you, where is here?"

"Where is here?" mused the walls. "Don't know that I can really answer that for you. That could mean anything, couldn't it? Is there a universal 'here'? Just 'here' from your point of view? Very interesting question—"

"Look, sorry, but who's talking?"

"I am."

"And who are you?"

"I am what I am. I'm everything in here. And I'm nothing really."

There was something about the style and tone of this conversation that was reassuring to Jules. It was very Theodore-like, and it suggested to him that he might be in the right place.

"Whose house is this?"

"It's the Earth Return Group House, of course, but at the moment it's leased to the Pines. There's Abraham, Hillary, and young Theodore. Although I haven't seem him for a day or two."

Jules felt a surge of happiness. He was here. Home! Theodore's home. He was in Fifteen Billion and Seventy-three.

"Ummm. I know where Theodore is."

"Do you now? Good for you."

"Yes. Don't you want to know?"

"Why would I want to know? I'm just a voice. I don't exist, you know."

"Right, OK. Ummm, I think his parents want to know."

"Abraham and Hillary? Yes, they might."

"Well, can I tell them? Do you know where they are?"

"No. They went out. Came back, looked terribly upset. Got out their JumpMans and took off. I haven't seen them since."

Of course, Jules thought. They're off searching for Theodore. But where would they look? As far as they knew, he could be anywhere and anywhen in the last fifteen billion years.

What to do?

Then he had an idea.

"Ummm, walls?" asked Jules tentatively.

"House actually, but yes, what do you want?" answered the house.

"Are there kitchen drawers in this room?"

"Do you mean perhaps the four kitchen drawers, one beneath the other with the knives and forks in the top and the things that are never used but are not to be thrown out in the bottom one?"

"Yes, that's them!" replied Jules.

"Why do you want them?"

"I need a piece of paper and a pen."

"A piece of paper?"

"Yes. Please."

"And a pen?"

"Yes. Please."

"What an extraordinary thing to ask for. And why would you think they'd be in a kitchen drawer today? The only surviving pieces of paper are in the City Museum along with seventeen red and green biros found in a kitchen drawer surviving from Mil 3. And you know what? None of the pens worked. They must have had a deep spiritual significance for people then, because they kept them. They didn't throw them away. What were you thinking of doing with them, anyway?"

"I need to leave a message for Theodore's parents."

"Well, speak up."

"I NEED TO LEAVE A MESSAGE—"

"Yes, I can hear you. In fact I've been recording you since you Jumped here. You are an intruder, you know. Every camera in the place has been on. If you want to leave a message, just speak up. I'll play it for them as soon as they get back."

Jules turned around, looking for a camera.

"Just look straight ahead," advised the walls. "I've got

you in a nice, medium close-up. Bit of lint or something on your T-shirt up near the neck, and just push your hair up in the front there? That's good and in five, four, three . . . you're on!"

"Mr. and Mrs. Pine? Hi, I'm Jules Santorini. You don't know me, but I'm a, well, I guess I'm a friend of Theo's. Of Theodore, your son. Anyway, look, I know where he is. He's really sorry he's a bit late, but he's sort of stuck at my friend Gen's place. He's been there for two days now and he won't come back to here. He's got a cold and says he doesn't want to risk everyone getting it. And he says his JumpMan is weird. By the way, he's visible. Present or whatever you say. I know I'm not meant to know any of this, but maybe you should just ignore all that and come and get him? He does seem pretty sick."

Giving Genevieve's address to some people who lived three thousand years in the future seemed a strange thing to be doing, and then Jules realized they'd need more than a house number and the name of a street to find them. So he told them the time and date as well.

"I know that's Old Time, but I hope you can make the conversion all right and come and find him. I'm sorry he's stuck in Mil 3, which Theodore seems to think is the worst time to be alive, so I hope you can come and get him really soon and I know he does too."

Jules was one of those people who never knew when to stop talking on a voice mail or answering machine, and then would spend just as long apologizing for taking up so much time as he did babbling on in the first place.

"Ummm, sorry, you can stop listening now, you've got all you need, there's nothing else worth hearing after this, except for me saying I hope to see you soon. Umm . . ."

"Yes, that's enough, I think I've got that," interrupted the house.

Jules felt a bit stupid.

"They'll get that all right?" he asked.

"Don't worry. First thing."

Jules wandered back into Theodore's room. As he did, a corner of the blind flapped open in the breeze. He went over to the window and pulled back the blind.

He looked out over forest as far as he could see. Dotted here and there were small groups of buildings, rising just above the trees. He looked down, and could see that he was about three or four floors up in a very slight kind of pole construction. The building was in a clearing and through the clearing ran a thin silver rail.

He let the blind drop and looked at the remote. Time to go, he thought. Hang on, he thought. I'm in Fifteen Billion and Seventy-three. I'm never going to come here again. I'm going to go back to my time without even sticking my head out the front door?

~ *Yes, said his brain. You are. Don't be a nong. Go home. Now.*

~ *Oh, come on, brain. Aren't you just a bit curious?*

~ *I am so curious that I want to leap out of your head and go and have a look myself, said his brain. But don't be an idiot. Don't you watch television? Isn't this what always happens? Hero completes mission, hero thinks, I'll just have one more little look over here, and whammo! The aliens attack!*

~ *There're no aliens here. Come on, we'll just stick our head out the front door.*

Jules's brain kept up its very sensible protests but Jules ignored it and he marched down the hall to where he thought the front door should be.

The hallway ended but there was no front door.

"Door?" he asked, feeling as though he was getting the hang of this house where nothing was visible but everything was possible.

"I'll need a password," said the house.

"House? It's me. The one who recorded the message? I'm the intruder, remember? I don't know the password. Why don't you let me out and then just don't let me back in?"

Nothing happened. Jules wondered if this was a thoughtful pause while the house considered his proposal, but then he realized that he was starting to regard the house as something that could think and make decisions, and that seemed ridiculous.

"I've thought about your proposal," replied the house. "It's a win–win all around really. Out you go."

The outlines of a door appeared, along with a handle that then turned itself and the door swung open.

"Don't tell anyone, oak eye?" the house asked as he walked through the open door.

Now that he could go outside, Jules was completely terrified. This was it, he wouldn't be able to get back in. Maybe he should just wait here. Maybe he should just press the Go button right now and head on home.

~ *Do it, urged his brain. Press the button!*

But then again, here he was in Fifteen Billion and Seventy-three. He'd left a message, Theo's parents were sure to get it, was he really going to go back to Gen's bedroom—fabulous bedroom though it might be—without even looking out the front door at the world of Theodore Pine?

~ *Yes! screamed his brain.*

Jules stepped outside.

The door closed and disappeared, and Jules was shut out of Theodore's house and walking into his world.

The day was sunny and pleasant, and the breeze that had been blowing through the house was gentle and warm. He was standing in a clearing in a forest. Around him were six other buildings about eight to ten stories high, similar in style to the Pines' building. They all seemed slight, like they were hardly there at all, and in many places there were no walls so he could look right in, to the bare rooms. There were people moving about in some of the buildings and Jules saw a table rise out of the floor and a man start to prepare a meal, taking ingredients out of a fridge that slid forward out of a paper-thin wall.

The forest ran right up to the edge of the clearing, and the buildings appeared to be constructed in natural openings in the trees. A creek burbled away to his left, and something largish scuttled off into the trees. The forest was thick and went on for as far as he could see. This was nothing like the bush on the outskirts of Jules's city. There, the bushland was full of rubbish and old car bodies, crisscrossed by tracks and generally kind of a dusty dispiriting place to visit. This forest looked like wilderness—thick, entangled, and untouched.

Directly in front of the Pines' building was a kind of car with two men in it. The car was a small pod, just a cabin really, and it sat on the silver rail that Jules had noticed from Theodore's window. The rail ran off into the trees.

A similar pod with a youngish woman in it emerged from a building opposite, slid smoothly over to the main rail in front of Jules, and then shot off into the forest.

Jules looked about the clearing and felt a bit disappointed. This was it? Three thousand years in the future and they lived in kind of pole apartment buildings and got around in little trams? He'd been hoping for jet cars and some kind of megacity that covered half the globe.

He didn't really take much notice when the two men got out of the pod in front of him and began walking toward him. One of them was short and plump and was smiling all over his face, the other was very large and ambled along behind the short one.

Both of them were very focused on Jules.

"Hi," said the short one. The large one nodded and looked round the clearing, as if he were checking for something.

"Any news on Theo?" asked the short one, then without waiting for Jules to answer went on, "You just came out? His Mum and Dad had any luck?"

"I don't know," said Jules nervously.

"You didn't talk to them?" asked the short one, all smiles and worry at the same time.

"They were TimeJumping," said Jules, hoping desperately that this was the right thing to say.

"Of course they were!" said the short one. "Oh, I can't imagine what they're going through. They must be going everywhere to try and find him. You know, Solly, I think we really are going to have to put some effort very quickly into this."

Jules was finding this conversation very strange. Of course it was strange. He was in another time, he was talking to people who seemed to know all about Theo and his disappearance from their time, and who seemed to be concerned about it. But the short one kept staring at the JumpMan and the big one, Solly, was now edging behind Jules as he kept up his habit of looking around while trying to look like he wasn't.

"You're a friend of his?" asked the short one.

"Yes," said Jules carefully.

"Oh, I'm sorry, I'm used to everyone knowing me. I'm Quincy Carter One, Cheeo of the TimeMaster Corporation. We make the JumpMan. That's a very interesting model you've got there, in fact. Where exactly did you get it?"

Quincy was leaning in very close to Jules. Solly was behind him now and leaning over the top of him.

"Do you know where Theo is?" asked Quincy so quietly Jules wasn't sure he'd heard him. But he was sure he didn't like the look in Quincy's eye, which was now a little too close to his own.

"You know where he is, don't you? You're the kid he's been Jumping with. We've seen the recording from Making of Fire, you know. That was you, right? Why don't we get in the pod and we'll go back to the office and talk about it, hmm?"

Jules was backed right up against Solly, who was resting a hand on his shoulder. As Quincy reached out to take the JumpMan, Jules pulled it away from him, just a few inches. A venomous look crossed Quincy's face and he hissed like a snake.

"Give it to me, kid!"

Jules darted sideways and ran.

Simple as that. When in doubt, run away. It worked with bullies at school, it worked with the Neanderthals. Jules now thought of it as the timeless solution to many problems, and he had every faith in it working here. Theodore had run like he'd never heard of running and Jules took a gamble that these two fellows would be the same.

They were. They flopped after him like a couple of seals, and within a few seconds Jules had run into the forest and lost them.

A few seconds later, he lost himself.

This was real forest. The trees were tall, the undergrowth was thick and in parts almost impenetrable. Vines hung everywhere, there were fallen logs, boggy bits, prickly bits, slicey bits, bits that tangled around his ankles, sticky bits, bits that got clogged in his hair and smeared his clothes. And none of them was remotely like a path or a road.

He kept on going, slogging through it all, and by the time he felt like he'd put enough distance between himself and Quincy and Solly, he was emerging into another clearing, just like the one he'd started from only about twice as large. This one had a taller, twenty-story building in the middle of it, with what looked like a viewing tower on the top. Jules could see people up there. He decided to go up and have a look around. If he didn't see anything or anyone that might be able to help him, then he'd Jump back to Theodore and Gen.

The doors to the building were open. He walked inside and in the middle he found conventional lift doors. There was a button. He pressed it and a few seconds later the doors opened. He got in, and pressed up. Just like home.

The lift stopped at the top, the doors opened, and he got out. The people who he'd seen up there were now waiting for the lift and as he got out, they got in. One couple glanced at his clothes but no one else took any notice of him. He was simply another kid with a JumpMan.

The place was empty. Jules took in the view. The tree canopy stretched to the horizon. Rolling green forest covering gentle hills in every direction. Every few miles there were clusters of buildings. Sometimes just six or eight, and then they encircled a larger cluster of perhaps twenty. In the middle of the larger ones were other towers like the one he was in. Far off in the distance he could see a larger group of buildings, perhaps a hundred or so, and several very tall towers, taller than the one he was in. All the buildings looked the same, almost not there at all, and as though they could open up, disappear, or become more solid on command.

The lift doors opened behind him. Quincy and Solly stepped out.

Jules knew he had only one option left. He closed his eyes and pressed the large round button of the remote.

chapter seven

Better Luck Next Time

Jules heard the sounds of a storm and the crashing of waves and felt warm rain on his skin before he even got around to opening his eyes. Not Gen's bedroom, was his first thought, as he gazed out on a turbulent grey-green sea that was throwing itself about underneath an equally turbulent sky. Thunderclouds were gathering at a speed usually only seen in cartoons and lightning was flashing about like the colors on Theodore's hair. The day was warm, and the rain, which fell on him as though somebody was pouring a bucket of water over him, was tepid. He wasn't frightened by this clash of elements all around him, but he was scared out of his wits to find that he wasn't back in Gen's bedroom about to tell Theodore and Gen what he'd done. He'd had enough adventures already, hadn't he? Did he need any more?

Where was he and, as he was now accustomed to thinking, when was he?

He was on a shore with nothing but rocks and crashing seas. The sea was a texture he'd never seen and the rocks looked new, all smooth and unweathered. They were strange colors as well, rusty yellows and bright browns and reds. The scene was familiar but it all looked kind of wrong. Jules started to understand exactly how Theodore must have felt when he opened his eyes and found himself in Gen's bedroom. Being lost anywhere was scary, but at least you usually knew what day it was. Being lost somewhere on the planet in the last fifteen billion years of time wasn't just scary. Jules felt like everything he'd ever thought was certain had just evaporated like a puddle in the sun.

Something had gone very wrong. He hadn't Jumped back to his own time, to the reassuring surrounds of Gen's bedroom. He could be stuck here forever, or he could try and Jump again and end up anywhere and anywhen.

Jules looked down at the screen on the remote. It read "First Fish." What did that mean?

He looked around. And saw the answer. A few yards in front of him, a fish head was sniffing the rocks.

Jules took a few steps forward. The fish head was attached to a long blueish body. The creature looked like something between a fish and an eel. It was pulling itself up the rocks with its fins. As it did so, it opened its mouth wide, as if astonished to find itself wandering around where it wasn't wet.

Jules wondered which of them felt more alarmed at finding themselves in this strange new world.

~ I think it's the fish out of water.

The fish ignored Jules and flopped past him toward a muddy pool, where it flopped in and made itself at home.

First Fish.

First fish to walk out of the ocean.

Jules was looking at the ultimate ancestor of all life on land. The first thing to leave the ocean and have a go at this Earth stuff. Without this fish–eel thing, no dinosaur, no elephant, no bird, no monkey, and no man.

Jules wanted to go and shake it by the fin.

It was all very fascinating, but not that fascinating that

Jules wanted to stay. What if he was stuck and he had to eat that social-climbing slug in the mud pool behind him? Could he undo the entire process of evolution because he'd come back in time a couple of billion years and needed a snack? Would it matter if he ate this particular one? Surely there was some other fish out there with ambition?

Jules knew he was starting to go mad. It was time to leave.

He sat on a rock for a while and studied the remote. It was in pre-set mode, but much as he scrolled up and down the options on the screen he couldn't seem to find a way out, or any reference to his year in the despised Mil 3. But then again, why would there be? Theodore being there was a big mistake. Still, thought Jules, there must be some record of it in this thing somewhere. They'd Jumped back there a few times already.

What to do?

There was nothing else to do.

He closed his eyes and pressed the Go button once more.

He opened his eyes. Or his eyes were opened for him. Or there were no eyes anymore. All was light. There was only light. He was light. He was still, totally motionless, but at a rate of thousands of miles every second. He was expanding in every direction. He was as tall as the universe and as wide as forever, and he felt as tiny as a proton's heart. This had been happening to him forever, but forever had only been happening for the last few seconds. He looked at the remote: "3 After BB," it read. That's it, he thought! Theodore had said it once. Three Seconds after the Big Bang.

So the entire universe had just been let out of the box and was now rushing by him. Or was he rushing with the universe, still so closely bound to all matter and energy that he couldn't distinguish himself, Jules Santorini, from the entire cosmos? He really couldn't see himself, he was simply more light in an everything of light, but it seemed he had a self so he must be around here somewhere. Looking down even though there was no up or down, through what he thought might be his feet, Jules could see a spot at the center of this brightness that was a little brighter than everything else. Jules wondered if that was it—the Big Bang.

So if you could go three seconds after the Big Bang, could you go three seconds before the Big Bang? *Was* there something before the Big Bang? Maybe, maybe not.

I mean, thought Jules, here I am. I am now the universe and I still can't figure this stuff out. What about time? Was there any time before the Big Bang, or did time start ticking away when everything else scarpered out of the box and headed for the infinite fringes of the universe? Who turned this thing on anyway?

~ *Could you think about something else? asked his brain. Better brains than I have been knocked out early on those questions. They're good questions, but could we think about this when we're perhaps tucked up in bed and not while we appear to be a stream of particles moving at the speed of light away from the Big Bang itself?*

~ *Reasonable proposition, thought Jules.*

And he closed what he felt might be his eyes and pressed the Go button.

Silence. Jules opened his eyes. He was in his kitchen.

His kitchen?

It was his kitchen. There was a bit of toast on the floor that he'd meant to clean up that morning. There was a soggy old teatowel draped over a chair. And there was his dad.

Definitely his kitchen. Whatever was wrong with this JumpMan it seemed determined to keep getting them back to this time. But now it was moving things a little up the road.

"Jules! Where the hell did you spring from? I just came home. You weren't here. I rang Katherine and got the maddest rave from her, but I gathered you were down there. I was about to go down there myself. And then you just appear out of nowhere in front of me. What's that thing you're hanging onto?"

Typical, thought Jules. I can get away from guys in Fifteen Billion and Seventy-three and I can survive the Big Bang, but I can't stop getting into trouble with Dad.

"Ummm," Jules said, really hoping that by the time he got to the end of ummm, his brain might have thrown a helpful excuse or two his way. But no, his brain was panicking and running around looking for a place to hide.

"Ahhhhhh." He tried really hoping that by the time he got to the last "h" he might have thought of something. But all he thought of was nothing again.

"Uhhhhhhhh," and round about the fourth "h" he did have an idea.

"Dad. There's a kid from three thousand years in the future. He's staying at Gen's place. He's really sick. I've just been to Fifteen Billion and Seventy-three to try to help him. I couldn't. I have to go right now and see what's happened. Bye, Dad."

Jules ran. Running had worked before.

As he reached the front door, he heard Tony call out

from the kitchen, but Jules just kept on going and ran as fast as he could to Gen's house.

He ran through the open front door and up the stairs and straight into Gen's room.

"Jules!" Gen leapt up from the bed where she was sitting holding Theodore's hand. "Oh, thank goodness you're back. You've been gone for so long and Theodore is getting really sick. Bits of him keep disappearing and take a look at his knees. Do you think they're fading?"

Theodore was pale and breathing in shallow little gulps, as though the air was too much for him. Were his knees fading away? Jules felt worn out from the pressure of having to make decisions.

"Theodore. Theo. I've been there. I've been to your place. The JumpMan's working. Why don't you just do it? Just Jump home! I've been there. The JumpMan's working. Just use it, you'll be fine." Jules thought he wouldn't worry Theodore with the details about the men chasing him, or his parents off TimeJumping, or the fact that to get back here he'd been via the First Fish and the Big Bang. Surely the most important thing was to get Theo back to Fifteen Billion and Seventy-three, and they'd be able to sort everything out there.

Theodore opened his eyes and spoke in a tired whisper. "Jules. Regular little TimeJumper now, eh? But you still don't get it. Not really. I can't just Jump back, Jules. I've got a disease. I can't risk bringing it back." Theodore closed his eyes, exhausted from talking.

"You've got a cold, Theo!" Jules was virtually yelling at him in distress and frustration. "It's not a disease, it's just a cold. You get over them in a day or two!"

"Maybe you're right. But we don't have them in my time. And who knows what it might do if I take this 'cold' thing back with me," said Theodore in a weak voice.

"People will sniffle, and you'll have to invent tissues. That's all. Nothing bad will happen. Oh please, will you just try a Jump?" pleaded Gen.

Theodore looked up at them both.

"You want me to go," he said in a pathetic little voice.

"No!" they cried together.

"Well, yes," said Gen a moment later. "You can't stay here like this."

Theodore closed his eyes for a moment.

"You're right. I have to try. I'll just have to go back home and see what happens. Who knows, it might work. Or I might end up home with no head. Can't be that bad."

Jules and Gen felt an enormous sadness come over them. Theo could stay here and fade away. Theo could Jump back and leave bits of himself across the next three millennia. It was a great choice.

"Theodore," said Gen. "Let's get someone. Let's tell my dad."

"Nip!" ordered Theo, suddenly energized. "That's the worst thing you could possibly do. If you people now get a JumpMan . . ." and Theo shuddered as if the idea of what Mil 3 people might attempt if they got a JumpMan was just too terrifying to even think about.

"Give me the JumpMan, Jules."

Jules shook his head and hugged the JumpMan to himself a little harder.

"Jules," said Theo quietly. "It's not even yours. Time to give it back."

Jules knew he was right. He handed it over.

Theodore flicked up the screen on the remote and pressed a couple of buttons.

He looked at the two of them and smiled.

"Thanks. For Mil 3 guys, you're not too bad."

He closed his eyes and pressed the Go button.

Theodore opened his eyes. Jules was hanging on to his legs and Gen had grabbed him around the neck.

"What are you doing? Are you two completely zongoid? I take it all back. You are as stupid as any other Mil 3 idiot!" Theodore yelled and then coughed violently.

"We just wanted to make sure you were OK," cried Gen.

"What does it matter? What could you have done anyway?" Theodore coughed loudly and lay down.

Gen looked desperately at Jules and then started to realize why he wasn't saying anything. This is a funny sort of home, she thought. She guessed from Jules's expression that they hadn't Jumped to Fifteen Billion and Seventy-three.

They were on a rock ledge on the side of a cliff, about 150 feet up. Above them jutted another ledge, shading them from the heat of the sun. The ledge was sandy and there were comfortable grooves in the cliff face to lean their backs against while they looked at the incredible view.

The cliff ran for miles in either direction and faced out onto a deep valley and across to another mountain range. Off to their right, maybe ten or twelve miles away, a smallish volcano was burping up ash and lava.

The valley below was thick with forest and they were sitting about level with the top of the tree canopy. Great vines entangled the huge branches of the trees, enormous flowers as big as umbrellas bloomed in thick masses in front of them filling the air with their honey scent, and below them grazed a herd of brachiosaurus. One of the dinosaurs stuck its head up in the air and seemed to catch a whiff of them. It bellowed and it was like someone had stuck a tuba over Jules's head and blown it as hard as they could.

Above them swooped a flock of pterodactyls. A flock? wondered Jules. Maybe that's the right word for pelicans, but it doesn't seem right for these things. Sharp-looking beaks, bits of bone sticking out of their wings, long claws hanging off the bottom of skinny little legs. They didn't resemble birds at all. More like half-starved sharks with wings.

~ *You know what they call a gang of crows, don't you?*

~ *What?*

~ *A murder.*

~ *A what?*

~ *A murder of crows. A gang of crows. It's called a murder.*

~ *How do you know that?*

~ *Actually, you know that. You've just forgotten. Lucky I'm here, really, or you wouldn't remember a thing.*

A murder of crows. This then is a slaughter of pterodactyls, thought Jules.

As if to balance the smoking volcano on one side of the view, to their left a waterfall plunged hundreds of feet off a ridge down into a lake. As they gazed out, a creature surfaced and swam about for a while. It looked familiar to Jules, with its small head and long neck sticking up out of the water. Two more loops of its body were visible above the water following along behind. It looked exactly like the kind of sea monster they used to draw on very old maps back when people believed they could sail off the edge of the world. Beyond the edge of the world they'd write something like, "Here Be Dragons!" and then draw something pretty much like what Jules was looking at now.

The place hummed with life. It was stunningly, breathtakingly beautiful. Plus it was the golden hour of the day; that moment when the sun is not yet setting but it's gone to its back door and yelled out to everyone that it's thinking about going down in the next half-hour or so.

Theodore stretched himself out on the sandy ledge and contemplated the view.

"I've never brought anyone here," he said. "It's my secret place. I found it and I was never going to show it to anyone."

"I thought you weren't allowed to go just anywhere?" said Gen.

"Nip, we're not meant to, but everyone does," he replied.

"How did you find this place?" asked Jules.

"Just luck. I was practicing for my SiteSearch Licence and I picked a space–time coordinate at random, and fell out of the sky above this. Made a few adjustments and landed back here. Since then, I've come here a lot, whenever I just want to be somewhere alone.'

Jules thought it was about the best secret hideout he'd ever seen. He'd have had more food and maybe a TV, but there was something to be said for not having anything like that. Sitting here watching the sunset and listening to the dinosaurs roar was pretty good.

"You know what?" said Theodore. "I think a lot of people have little spots like this. Some place that they think of as just theirs. You know, right now, we are the only humans on the entire planet. You want to get away from it all—try going back one hundred and fifty million years."

Theodore sneezed. The particle dropouts had stopped, but he had no energy. The vibrant curiosity, the constant stream of observations and jokes had stopped. His Coat hadn't spoken a word all day and as for his hair . . .

"Is that your natural hair color?" asked Gen.

"Is it mousey brown?" mumbled Theodore.

"Uh-huh," replied Gen.

"That's it. See why I love Molecule Follicle Gel?"

They fell silent for a while. The Sun was setting behind the volcano. The ash-filled sky was purple, gold, pink, and red, and the Sun was a brass ball in the center of it. Above it, high streaks of cloud trailed like crimson ribbons.

"You were planning to come here and . . . and . . ." Jules couldn't complete the sentence. "Are you ever going to Jump home?"

"I can't go home, Jules, and I didn't want to stay in Mil 3."

Despite his concern and worry for Theodore, Jules felt a surge of anger. Here we go again, he thought. He's dying and he's still got enough go in him to bag us out.

"Theo, what is the whole thing with Mil 3? Are we that bad? I've been to your time, remember, and it didn't look so great."

Theodore looked sadly at them. "I may as well tell you. What does it matter?" He shrugged. "You've Jumped, you know it all anyway, and your chances of getting back from here are pretty slim."

He lifted himself up on one elbow. "In twenty-five years time, the world ends."

Jules and Gen waited for a moment.

"And?" asked Gen.

"And?" replied Theodore. "There's no 'and' after the world ends. The world ends."

"But you're here," said Jules. "And I've been to the world in three thousand years time. It's still going on then."

"Yeah, well, all right, it didn't completely end, but it gets into a lot of trouble. There's the whole environment thing for a start. For example, did I ever tell you what you have to do to get your TimeJumper's Licence?"

Jules and Gen shook their heads.

"You've got to go to a JumpSite called the Journey of the Last Whale. It's a very important site. It's just a few years in the future from your time, and it's on an iceberg in the Southern Ocean, a hundred or so miles from Antarctica. Cold. I wasn't really dressed for it, I admit, but I was pretty sure The Coat'd cope."

"All weathers, from minus 15 to plus 50, PromoCloth coats are there for you."

"Shut up, Coat," they all said together. Theodore resumed his tale.

"Anyway, up comes the last whale. The seas are enormous, not like big waves, but an enormous rolling swell—seems like a mile from the top of it to the bottom. It's freezing cold and you just sit there and wait and watch the birds pull up strange-looking fish and circle about crying in the wind."

Theodore coughed a little and looked out across the valley. He was talking very quietly and Gen and Jules moved in a little closer. The stegosaurus had settled down and the brachiosaurus had stopped trumpeting like they were all keen to hear his story.

"When the whale comes up, it's like his big eye is

staring straight at you. Like he knows you're there. Seems to take minutes for his enormous body to come out of the ocean and when he crashes back in, he creates his own swell as big as any of the waves rolling by.

"Just behind him are a couple of guys in a little run-about boat. Behind them is a bigger ship. They're whale researchers and experts and they want to know why whales are suddenly disappearing. Numbers had built up for a while, but now, in a couple of years, they've gone down again.

"So they harpoon this whale. Kill it, haul it into the ship, slice it up and study it. Must be something wrong with the whales. Better kill one and try to find out what's going wrong. They didn't know it was the last one. The researchers thought there was more. They thought they needed just one more to study to find out what was going on. But no one ever saw a whale again."

The silence became deep as Jules and Gen absorbed Theodore's words.

"Did everything die? The whales and the fish and the birds and everything?" Gen asked eventually in a shocked tone.

"Nip. We're not even certain that all the whales died. Because a few years after that everyone started leaving."

Jules and Gen just looked at him.

"I said everyone started leaving."

"Leaving the cities?" asked Gen.

"Nip, leaving the planet," said Theodore.

There was a pause again. As so often happened with Theodore, he'd say these things like he was saying everyone went out for an afternoon stroll, and so it took a moment or two to really understand what he'd just said.

"Umm, where did they go?" asked Jules, sure that this was a stupid question.

"That's the next question, Jules, very good," said Theodore. "They went to Mars."

"Everyone went to Mars?" asked Gen.

"Well, not quite everyone. Look, the thing about Mil 3 is this. Right at the start of the new millennium, the rich started getting richer. Really rich. You know, some Indian princes, and kings and queens and such had been rich, but in Mil 3, once you got rich, there was no stopping you. The rich started to get ridiculously rich. And the poor, well, if you're poor, you're poor, that's about it. Anyway, the rich started to retreat into big compounds and then whole suburbs, and soon there were entire states and big slices of the nice bits of everywhere that were only for the rich. But the rich being the rich, always seemed to want more. So the rich decided to move the poor on. They got rid of them."

"What?" said Gen and Jules together. "That's terrible."

"Ah, no, this is the good bit. See, the rich would decide that they wanted, say, all of California. As well, they needed new things to be rich with. So they found a whole new planet. They started investing in Mars. Vast sums of money. The Mars boom was extraordinary. People made fortunes so then there were more rich people. As they got Mars going, they started to shift people up there. Like I said, once they decided they wanted all of California, they had to do something with the people. And all the poor people and the ordinary people who were so sick of the rich wanting everything, and owning everything and taking everything and doing it all right in everyone's face, were queueing up to go to Mars."

"You're making this up," said Gen.

"Nip, this is what happened. Before too long there were only rich people left on Earth. Everyone else was up on Mars, having a great time."

"Why didn't the rich people want to go to Mars?"

"They thought there was no one up there they'd like. So they stayed on Earth, built bigger and bigger houses, with bigger and bigger pools and garages for all their cars, and eventually they found they owned everything, but no one really cared anymore. And then one day, the richest man in the world came downstairs and found his fridge wasn't working. He tried to find someone to fix it, but the last fridge mechanic had gone to Mars the day before. Someone else couldn't find anyone to get their breakfast. The rich were all alone. No one to do the work. The garbage piled up, they'd forgotten how to cook things and look after themselves, and so they all just faded away. No one on Mars cared. It wasn't like we missed them. It was about a thousand years before anyone thought, haven't heard much from Earth lately. By then they'd gone."

Around them everything was quiet. A deep violet dusk had settled over the valley. Their faces were lit with a faint red from the glow of the distant volcano, and the moon was rising over the waterfall. Stars were starting to come out in thick clusters above them. At nighttime Theodore's hideaway was possibly even more beautiful.

"So, yip, it was fantastic," Theodore continued. "Everyone got on really well, there was so much to do to get the place working that everyone forgot about making money and all that stuff. The only way to survive was to work together to mine the water, and work the solar energy mills to create atmosphere and environments and all the rest. Humans have only just returned to Earth. In Fifteen Billion and Seventy-three there's only a few million people living here. And we're under strict controls not to mess the place up again."

"So is everyone going to come back to Earth?" asked Jules.

"No, they don't want to. Mars is great."

"Wow, I'd love to see it."

"Me too. I've never been there." Theodore looked sad. "Guess that's not going to happen now."

They sat quietly again for a while thinking sad thoughts.

"So, anyway," resumed Theodore. "That's why we think the start of the third millennium Old Time is a really stupid time. You did some really dumb things."

Jules and Gen studied the ground and became very interested in how many grains of sand were in front of them.

"Sorry," mumbled Jules.

"I'm really sorry," said Gen.

"Thanks," said Theodore. "I'll make sure everyone for the next three thousand years gets to hear that."

They fell silent. Something large was snuffling through the forest below them.

"Theodore," said Jules. "Where is the past? Where's the future? When is the present?'

Theodore looked at Jules in surprise and then a slow smile spread across his face.

"Well done, Dodoboy," but he said it in a friendly way. "You know what you've just done?"

Jules shook his head.

"You've just qualified for your TimeJumper's Licence."

"What did I do?" Jules looked mystified.

"Asked the three essential questions of TimeJumping."

"That's all you have to do?"

"Yip, but *you* have to ask them. No one ever tells you that they're the questions. The day you ask them for yourself, is the day you're allowed to start Jumping solo."

Jules burst with pride.

"And?" he asked.

"And what?" replied Theo.

"The three most essential questions, are there three essential answers? Or do I have to figure them out for myself?"

"Nip, figuring out the question is always much harder than the answer." Theodore smiled and then declared, "The Past Is Gone, The Future's Unknown, The Present Never Happens."

Gen looked from Theo to Jules and back again a few times.

"What are you two talking about? What do you mean, The Present Never Happens? This is the present. Now."

"Well, no, that's now the past and this is the present. Now. Oops, there it goes again. Back into the past. Say now, Gen."

"No!" said Gen. "I won't."

"See, The Future's Unknown. I thought you'd say it!" said Theodore. "Like I say, The Present Never Happens—we just live with a lot of nows one after another."

Jules smiled to himself. He'd figured most of that out in the shower. When was that, just a day or so ago. He knew he was millions of years in the past, but he had no idea anymore what *time* it was. In the 3:15 PM sense of time. He also couldn't believe that Gen was having trouble with this. Hadn't she been the one arguing with Theo about time back when he'd first showed up? Jules looked out into the start of the night and felt pretty good, although it did cross his mind that there seemed to be a very large shadowy shape at the edge of the ledge that probably shouldn't be there. The large shadowy shape made a loud snorting noise, and Gen and Theo looked up as well.

The shadowy shape came closer and in the last bit of daylight they could see that it was an extremely large head. It had a long snout, and its upper teeth protruded out over its bottom lip. Two gigantic brown eyes were looking at them, and when it sniffed, it all but sucked them toward it.

"Theodore, is that what I think it is?" yelled Gen.

"Oh my DNA!" yelled Theodore. "T-Rex! I thought I was high enough to avoid them."

"Maybe them. But not him. Let's Jump!" yelled Jules.

"Jump? Are you crazy? We're fifty yards up!" said Theodore.

"TimeJump, you idiot!" yelled Jules.

"Oh! Good idea."

They leapt on the JumpMan, clung to one another, closed their eyes, and Jules pressed the Go button.

They opened their eyes.

Gen's bedroom again.

"We all here?" asked Gen, standing up very cautiously and hoping that they hadn't jumped a T-Rex back into her room by accident.

"Uh-huh," said Jules.

Theodore, however, was unconscious.

"Theo!" cried Gen.

They slapped his face and yelled at him, but he remained out of it.

Jules stood up.

"We've got to get help."

"No!" pleaded Gen. "Mum and Dad'll never understand."

"It's too late. He's not going to make it. How will you explain it to them if he, he . . ."

Jules went to the bedroom door and opened it, and then stopped with the door open.

"Gen!" he hissed. "Get over here!"

At the bottom of the stairs, they could hear Katherine talking to someone.

"Who did you say you were?" she was asking.

"I'm Abraham Pine and this is my wife, Hillary," a man replied. "We believe our boy Theodore came over to play after his Learning Session?"

"Who?"

"Theodore. Ted. Ed. Theo. Eddie?" Now it was a woman speaking. "Kids, eh?" she continued. "They come, they go. Bring home all sorts with them. Hard to keep up, isn't it? Are you Katherine Corrigan?" she asked.

"Yes."

"Oh, Theo's always talking about you. Shall we go and find him? He came here after a Learning Session?"

"A what?" Katherine sounded almost chirpy. Having gone completely mad she now accepted that strange things would keep happening to her, so the sudden appearance of two people dressed in peculiar clothes and making no sense whatsoever seemed completely normal to her.

"Learning Session. Perhaps I mean 'Mind Growth'?"

"Huh?"

"School?"

"School!"

"School, then. Did Theodore come here after school?"

Upstairs, Jules grabbed Gen by the arm. "It's his parents!

His mum and dad. They've come to pick him up!"

"How are we going to get them up here?"

"Oh come on, Gen. Katherine's so confused she won't even notice. Quick, get down there and bring them up here!"

Gen bolted down the stairs. Jules went to the top of the stairs and watched.

"Hi, Mr. Pine. Hello, Mrs. Pine." Gen waved and chatted cheerily like the Pines had been coming by for years. "I'm Gen. We met the other day, remember? Theodore's still working on our project for school, but I know he'd love to show it to you. Why don't you come on up?"

The Pines took the hint and they barged in past Katherine and up the stairs toward Gen's room.

"Hello, Mr. Pine. Mrs. Pine," said Jules.

They both looked startled and then they recognized Jules.

"You're the one who was at our house!" said Mr. Pine.

"That's me. I'm Jules," said Jules.

"Unbelievable. You TimeJumped. To tell us about our boy," said Mrs. Pine.

"Well, we didn't know what else to do," said Jules modestly.

"You did exactly the right thing. But it was incredibly dangerous. We can never thank you enough. We kept getting reports about Theodore. You were sighted at the Building of the Great Pyramid and at the Making of Fire. Code Cops are going crazy about having to fix up all those sites, but we could never find where you were Jumping back to. Thanks for the address."

Jules was feeling pretty good about them describing him as courageous and doing exactly the right thing in front of Gen, and he nodded in what he hoped was an even more modest kind of way.

"You better come in, he's pretty sick." Jules took them into the bedroom.

Mrs. Pine rushed across the bedroom to Gen's bed where Theodore was lying unconscious. From her pocket she drew out a small pencil-shaped device. She pressed it to his temples and Theodore's eyes flew open immediately.

"What? What? Oh nip! I'm not still here, am I? Mummy!" he yelled when he caught sight of her, and then tried to tone his excitement down. "Oh yip, hi. Hi, Dad. How are you? Good Jump?"

"We have been so worried. What went wrong?"

"I don't know. I've been visible—Oh great nanos, you two are as well."

"It's all right," Mr. Pine assured Theodore. "We took Jules's message to TimeMaster headquarters and Quincy

Carter was very understanding. In fact, he and Solly Booloo want to see you as soon as you get back."

At the mention of Quincy Carter and Solly Booloo, Jules frowned a little.

"Those people you mentioned. Quincy and Solly. I met them."

"You met them? Where?" asked Mr. Pine.

"Outside your house. They were a bit weird."

"Oh, well that's understandable. This has been the biggest thing ever. We haven't lost a TimeJumper since little Willy Gates went off."

"That's right, I remember that," said Mrs. Pine. "Wonder what happened to him."

Theodore started explaining what had happened to little Willy Gates and Jules kept quiet. He didn't remember Quincy and Solly as being all that understanding.

"Is Theo going to be all right?" asked Gen.

"Sure," said Mr. Pine. "We can Jump him back with our JumpMan and he'll be just fine."

"But we've got to do it now," said Mrs. Pine. "We've given him a particle retriever, but we better Jump soon while it's still at full strength."

Gen and Jules and Theodore all looked at one another.

"Sorry about everything," said Jules.

"Sorry we're such lousy Mil 3 types," said Gen.

Theodore stood there for a moment and then burst into tears and then rushed over and hugged them both.

"I'm sorry, I'm sorry. You two were great! I've been scared, so scared, I just didn't know what to do. I'll never be nasty about Mil 3 people again!"

"Yeah, you will, but just leave us out of it, OK?"

They stood holding hands, crying and laughing together.

"Gotta go," said Mr. Pine quietly.

Theodore stood back and joined his parents. He picked up his JumpMan and turned it off.

"Bye, guys. It's been amazing. I'll tell everyone in Fifteen Billion and Seventy-three about you."

"Bye, Theodore. We won't tell anyone about you."

The Pines grinned and nodded, and then in exactly the same instantaneous way that Theodore had first appeared, they vanished.

At that precise moment, the door opened and in walked Katherine, Cynthia, and Jules's dad.

"Right, there you are," said Jules's dad in the tone of a very old-fashioned father. "I've had about enough of this. I want to know what's going on and I want to know now."

"Where did they go?" asked Katherine.

"Who?" replied Gen, looking around her innocently.

"The couple. The ones who said their kid was here. You came down and got them, and said he was here doing his homework." Katherine's cheery surface cracked and her eyebrows started to twitch.

"Homework!" exploded Tony. "I never want to hear that word again!"

"Oh, that couple," said Gen. "They had to go."

"Go where? Where go?" Katherine cracked completely.

"Home." Gen was a picture of honesty.

"They couldn't have. I was at the door. Tony turned up. We haven't left. We came straight up the stairs. Cynthia was there the whole time."

"No, they went," said Jules. "We said good-bye and they were in a hurry and off they went."

Cynthia could contain herself no longer.

"They've had a kid from the future here all week! He was called Theo and he could go anywhere! He had a time-leaper or a jumper or a thing that you just pointed at and they've been going there. He was really weird and had weird hair and his coat could be a Barbie dress and they were going to let me wear it!"

Katherine shivered and one of her eyes rolled sideways while the other remained on her younger daughter. Jules and Gen stood there and looked at everyone with innocuous smiles on their faces. Suddenly Katherine barked like a dog at them, then grabbed Cynthia by the arm and hauled her out of the room.

Tony stood looking at them for a while.

"Should I bother asking what's really been going on?"

"Actually, Cynthia was telling the truth, Dad," said Jules.

"You're grounded. For a very long time. Possibly forever," said Tony.

Jules hung his head. He'd been expecting this but it was still annoying. Here he was getting punished for helping—no, hang on, *saving* a kid's life—and what had that kid ever done for him apart from sneer at him and try to steal his girlfriend?

~ *You did get to go three thousand years into the future, his brain reminded him.*

~ *Oh, sure, but now Dad's never going to trust me again, countered Jules.*

"I don't know what to do with you, mate," Tony said. "You've really gone ratty this week. Is this just a one-off, or is it the start of a whole rebellious kill-your-father stage? Should I worry, or should I let it go? I give you a bit of a go and you let me down every time." Tony was sad and confused. Not one of his fathering theories was working.

"I'm sorry, Dad," said Jules. "There was a lot going on this week."

"Mr. Santorini, it's my fault." Gen stepped bravely forward. "I kept asking Jules to help me with my homework and we just kept losing track of . . . time."

Jules had to stop himself from laughing out loud. We

didn't *lose* track of time at all, he thought. We *found* it!

Tony was talking again.

"Yeah, well, nice try, Gen. I don't remember any 'homework' that was ever that fascinating, so until further notice, you're under house arrest, Jules. 'Night, Gen. Say goodnight, Jules."

Jules smiled at Gen, grateful for her attempt, and headed out the door behind his dad.

"See you, Jules," she said. "We'll have to go to the movies some other time."

The door closed behind him.

She just said yes! Yes, she would go to the movies with him. She'd heard him the first time. And now where was he? On the wrong side of her door and grounded for the next three years.

~ *Yeah, but she said yes, said his brain.*

~ *She did, didn't she? said Jules. Didn't she?*

~ *She did.*

Jules floated down the stairs. His heart was light with relief, although his stomach was starting to flutter nervously. She'd said yes, so now he'd actually have to go through with it.

~ *Excuse me, said his brain. You have been alone with the first creature to walk on this planet, you've outwitted a dozen Neanderthals intent on killing you, and you're scared of going to the movies?*

~ Terrified, said Jules.

~ Don't blame you, said his brain.

Downstairs, Katherine was nowhere to be seen. A red-eyed Cynthia was curled up in the corner of the couch looking like she might sulk for the rest of the year. She shot them a bitter glance as they let themselves out.

Tony and Jules walked down the road together.

"Things are going to have to change," said Tony. "Bedtimes, coming and going. I want to see your homework every night. I've been too slack . . ."

Jules wasn't listening. He looked up at the stars. Millions of stars spread out above him. Not as many as could be seen away from the city, or say a hundred thousand years ago at a Neanderthal camp, but still a lot. Was it only a few hours ago he'd seen the Big Bang, the beginning of everything around him? Of all the stars and planets and of all the stuff in between? Had he really experienced the beginning of the universe? Where was it? How could he be here now, walking up the road with his dad banging on about how much trouble he was in, and then instantly be taken back fifteen billion years to the very beginning, when his dad was just a lot of hot gas?

Hasn't changed that much, thought Jules.

~ Very funny, said his brain.

Was it only a few hours ago that he'd been wandering

around Theodore's world, a world that wouldn't exist for another three thousand years? Except it existed *now*, because he'd just been there and Theodore and his parents were back there *now*.

~ *Stay with the jokes, will you, suggested his brain. All that* now *stuff makes me ache all over.*

Jules felt overwhelmed with all the questions. Where *was* Fifteen Billion and Seventy-three? Somewhere up there in the stars? Somewhere alongside him right now?

Would he ever see Theo again? Do people really go to Mars in just a few years from now? All that stuff Theo said about what was going to happen to Earth, what should he do about that? And just when would he and Gen get to go to the movies?

Jules yawned. It's funny, he thought. I know the future, but I don't know what's going to happen. It's true, what Theodore said: The Past Is Gone, The Future's Unknown, The Present Never Happens. Although, as he tuned into Tony still going on about the new rules and trust and what was expected from Jules from now on, he felt like the present and the future were looking pretty ordinary for the next few months at least.

Oh, what's going to happen to me? he wondered.

~ *You'll find out soon enough, replied his brain in an unusually kind and considerate tone. It's all just a matter of time.*

James Valentine is a broadcaster with 702ABC Sydney. He presents a news/talk shift each weekday afternoon from 1 PM. He writes and performs satirical radio comedy for *Humour Australia*, which is heard across the country on ABC Radio. He is also the presenter/producer of *The Screening Room*, a weekly program on contemporary cinema seen each Saturday night on *Showtime*. *JumpMan Rule #1* is his first children's novel.

James has written for *Rolling Stone*, *Vogue*, and *Cleo*. He was a music reviewer for *The Australian* and has written feature and opinion pieces for the *Sydney Morning Herald*.

His media career began with ABC Television where he presented *The Afternoon Show*, a daily program for children. He then worked for *Good Morning Australia*, before becoming host and writer of *TVTV*, a show that reviewed television.

James studied music at Melbourne State College and began working in jazz and rock bands. He played saxophone and woodwinds with Jo Camilleri, Kate Ceberano, and Stephen Cummings before joining the Models. With them he recorded two number-one hits, several platinum albums, and toured the United States and Europe. He went on to play with Absent Friends and Wendy Matthews.

James has two young children, Ruby and Roy, with his wife, Joanne, a psychologist. He wonders what it's like to have spare time.

CHECK OUT AN EXCERPT FROM

JAMES VALENTINE'S

JUMPMAN

RULE #2: DON'T EVEN THINK ABOUT IT

PRESENT NOW

FRIDAY NIGHT ▲ EARLY MIL 3

Jules leaned forward. How do you know if a girl wants to kiss you?

~ *You don't,* said his brain.

~ *So what if she doesn't want to kiss me?*

~ *That you'll know.*

Jules was standing on the porch of Gen's house. Gen's face was about half an inch away from his.

Everything had gone perfectly. The handholding had been a huge success: Gen's hand had stayed in his for about twenty minutes until, with a gentle smile, she'd finally let go.

After the film they'd walked quietly back to the train station, somehow falling into step in perfect rhythm and with a kind of swaying movement that meant they knocked against each other a lot. They'd talked about the last three months, how over the top their parents had been, how bizarre the whole thing was, how it was all starting to seem like some kind of dream. Were they really visited by Theodore Pine Four? Had Gen really gone to watch a Pyramid being built? Had Jules been to the future and then back to the Big Bang itself? They laughed at the way they were now really interested in history and were reading lots of books. Jules had started to tell Gen the story about how some archaeologists digging through the ruins of ancient Pompeii had discovered a pair of modern sneakers under a bed, and Gen had finished it off. She'd read it in the paper as well. There was great debate as to whether it was a prank and how anyone could have put a pair of shoes in a room that hadn't seen the light of day for two thousand years. Jules had wished they could just keep on walking and talking like this forever.

But they'd had to catch the train and get back home.

And now here they were, standing together on Gen's front porch with five minutes to spare, and it was time to say good night.

~ *She's not moving,* Jules said to his brain.

~ *That's good.*

~ *I'm going to do it all wrong.*

~ *Probably. But look, I'm your brain, right? I've watched you learn a lot of things. I remember trying to get your chubby little fingers to pick up blocks. And then toilet training—*

~ *Yeah, okay, can we go over this some other time? I think it's about to happen.*

Jules had a moment of panic, worse than he'd felt when he'd been lost in the future or when he was being chased by Neanderthals in the past.

~ What do I do? Does she know what to do?

~ Maybe. You' ll need to tilt your head to one side.

~ What?

~ The nose. You have to make some room for the nose.

~ Which side? Left?

~ Sure. Tilt your head to the left.

~ No, right. I'm going to go right.

~ Okay. Right.

~ I'm not sure.

~ DO IT NOW!

Jules went left. Gen turned her head a little to her left as well. He was staring into her eye. Gen smiled at him, looked down, back into his eyes, and then just moved her head forward a little, closing her eyes as she did.

Jules could feel the heat of her face, and a soft, warm smell wafted up his nostrils that made him feel lightheaded and powerful all at once.

Opening his mouth and licking his lips—he screamed.

Gen leaped back, like he'd bitten her on the nose. Then she screamed as well.

Standing next to them was a thin, bony man with a long, weathered face. His eyes were intense and they flicked back and forth from Gen to Jules like a lizard choosing which fly to eat for breakfast. His clothes looked like he'd been wearing them for weeks. And he was standing just a little too close for comfort.

"Sorry," he said, scratching a bit and looking nervously about. "This is not a good time. I'll go away and come back earlier."

"You! I know you." Gen was still screaming. Then her voice dropped to a hiss. "You're that guy. Franklin!"

Franklin? thought Jules. Who's Franklin? How did he just appear like that? And why, instead of experiencing my first real live kiss with a real live girl, am I being interrupted by him? And why does Gen know who he is? And why does he smell bad? And why—

But Jules stopped asking himself questions because the strange, skinny, smelly guy was asking him one. "Who are you? Go home. I need to talk to her."

"Can you keep your voice down?" ordered Gen. "What are you doing here, Franklin? And why do you TimeJumpers always appear so suddenly?"

"How else are we going to appear?" shrugged Franklin. "Bit hard to make an appointment from three thousand years in the future."

"You're a TimeJumper!" said Jules. "From Fifteen Billion and Seventy-three?"

Franklin grabbed him by the arm and put his face up close to his. "Who are you? How do you know so much?"

"Owww!" Franklin's long, bony fingers and nails were digging into Jules's arm. "I'm, I'm Jules. I've Jumped. Who are you? Are you a friend of Theo's?"

At the mention of Theo's name, Franklin dropped Jules's arm and cast more nervous glances about. He scuttled out into the darkness and then back into the pool of light on the porch.

Staring at them, he muttered and tapped his teeth. Then he beckoned them into a huddle, and casting another glance over his shoulder, he said, "Know where I can get a little TimeHacking action? Hip me to it, huh? Maybe you know someone who knows someone?" This was accompanied by lots of winks and nods and fingers on the side of the nose.

Jules hadn't heard of TimeHacking. But he had heard of TimeJumping, and last time he'd done it there'd been a JumpMan, a hovering silver sphere with a red remote. Franklin didn't seem to have one.

"Where's your JumpMan?" Jules asked.

"JumpMan?" Franklin all but spat. "What, you think I'd use one of Quincy's little toys?" And he pulled back a filthy sleeve to reveal a sleek panel as thick as a biscuit and molded to his arm.

Jules looked at Franklin's device in amazement. Like Theo's JumpMan, it didn't have much on it—just a screen and a couple of buttons. But somehow in there was enough computing power to send a person or two anywhere and anywhen there was a decent JumpSite. From the Big Bang till yesterday. Fifteen billion years of history to explore. No wonder JumpMans were popular. From where Franklin and Theo had come, three thousand years in the future, a future where they calculated the date from the beginning of time, every kid had one. Come the weekend, no one was home—they were all having a fantastic time watching a Maori War Party go into action, or Marching with Napoleon to Moscow, or—for the more refined—watching Mozart Compose or perhaps enjoying a Day with Da Vinci. And they all did it with TimeMaster JumpMans.

Jules took a closer look. On the screen of Franklin's JumpMan he could read Gen's address and the date. It seemed like Franklin had meant to come here.

"This is a JumpMan, my friend, if you must use that term," Franklin said with a sneer. "I wanted to call them a Temporal Tempter but, as usual, Quincy got his way. Oh no, this," and Franklin tapped the device on his arm, "is not one of those pathetic, overwired coconuts Quincy has turned into a fashion accessory and flogged off to the kids. This uses my own Franklin Nixon ChronoMatic Lock Sequencer, Pre- and Post-Particle Oscillating Search Transfer System, and it calculates not just the distance from the Big Bang but also the distance from the next Universe Renewal Cycle, giving you WhenLock Accuracy that is beyond anything copycat Quincy has ever come up with. The Quantum Computers in this little wizz—"

"Franklin," Gen interrupted. "That's fascinating, but the last time I saw you, you were trying to grab one of those overwired coconuts off Theo and me! Which would have left us stranded forever at the Great Pyramid. And then you just disappeared. What are you doing here? What do you want? And can you keep it down a bit? Do you want everyone to hear you?"

Franklin shrugged. "Oh, yip, yip, sorry about that. I was a bit desperate. There's only so much sand and sun worship you can stand. You want to know what happened? Quincy Carter One's what happened. He Jumped me out. Now he wants to get rid of me again. But let's get down to it. I need to move a little Time about. Hack it. Sack it. Piggyback it. Know what I'm saying?"

Jules and Gen had no idea what he was saying. They both just wanted him to say it a little more quietly.

Then Franklin bent forward and peered into their faces. "So what happened to *you*?" he demanded.

Gen stepped back. "Franklin! What is going on? I've got no idea what you're talking about. What are you doing here? You don't make any sense and I want you to leave. You're going to get us into trouble! Go on, just JumpOff or Back or Hack or whatever you do. I don't know that I want anything to do with TimeJumping again. All it's done so far is ruin my life."

Good for you Gen, thought Jules. Let's get rid of him.

Wasn't this the same as last time? As soon as he got close to Gen, bang! Someone from Fifteen Billion and Seventy-three dropped by to ruin everything. Couldn't Franklin come back tomorrow? Or not at all?

"All right, all right." Franklin backed off a little. "Just take a quick peeky boo at this, Oak Eye?"

Franklin smoothed an area on the front of his Coat. Franklin's Coat was so ragged and filthy, Jules hadn't realized it was a Coat like the one Theo had worn. Now Franklin rubbed some dirt off the front panel, and a screen appeared, accompanied by a soft fanfare. Jules was impressed. The quality of the graphics and sound was very good.

"Welcome to HyperCoat AV Presentations," Franklin's Coat said in a full, creamy voice. "Please select from the following options. To view anything experienced in the last three hours, please say 'Three Hours'—"

"Yip, zip it, Coat," barked Franklin. "The Theo stuff, just play the Theo stuff."

"I'm sorry," replied the Coat. "Did you say the Leo stuff? For Astrology, just say your star sign—"

"Aaaargggh! It was easier with papyrus and bits of sharp metal! These Coats! They do everything except what you want them to do! Theo, Theo, Theo, get me the Theo grabs I clicked into five minutes ago, you useless piece of rag."

Jules wished Franklin would hurry up. But still, here was someone from the future who had a Coat with video. It was worth a look. He just didn't want to get caught, because this time, they wouldn't be grounded. This time, they'd be sent to boarding schools far away, run by obscure religious orders who believed in cold showers and regular beatings as a way of keeping young people in check.

"Umm, Gen," Jules ventured, thinking to suggest that Franklin might come back at a more convenient time.

But Gen wasn't listening. She was watching Theo on the *Hurrah Banter Show* on the screen on Franklin's Coat. Jules took a closer look. There was the back of Theo's gorgeous designer HyperCoat, complete with a huge handstitched TimeMaster logo. There were thousands of people, and you could sense the enormous excitement Theo generated as he walked into the room. Jules was amazed at how confident and experienced Theo appeared. He did all the things talk show guests always do and seemed to be doing it very naturally, like he'd been doing it forever. His hair looked amazing, and he was chatting with the host like they were old friends. Jules leaned forward a little to hear what they were saying.

Hurrah was talking. ". . . three months since you escaped from Mil 3, where a gang of TimeHackers using a primitive JumpMan kidnapped you and were threatening to let you fall apart unless you showed them how the new JumpMan Pro really worked. You didn't and—thanks to Quincy Carter One—you were rescued . . ."

"What did she just say?" blurted Gen.

"She said you were a ruthless gang of TimeHackers," said Franklin.

"We didn't kidnap him!" said Gen indignantly. "He just turned up in my bedroom and then he couldn't go home."

"I knew you weren't TimeHackers," said Franklin. "Why does everyone believe that story? Look where we are—it's Mil 3. Giddy clones, is that a lightbulb?" Franklin squinted up at the light over the porch. "Zip, you probably *know* Edison, right? Zif you're going to be TimeHacking. You don't even know what Time is. Nip, worse, you don't even know what *time* it is!"

He snorted. "It's Mil 3," he yelled. "Go inside the house. There'll be little clocks blinking everywhere and they'll all have different times on them!"

How does he know that, thought Jules, thinking of the clocks in his own kitchen. The one on the oven hadn't moved at all since it became a home for cockroaches, the one in the microwave was set on summer time, and the one in the radio was seven minutes slow. His watch was usually kind of close. . . .

"Zif they could have kidnapped Theo!" Franklin was chuckling and dancing about a little.

Gen was still watching Theo on the screen. "Are they making out he's some kind of hero or something?" She looked up at Franklin. "What's going on? Is Theo all right?"

"Huh, is Theo all right?" repeated Franklin. "He's more popular than breathing. The entire Two Planets have gone pineapple about him. He's on everything, he's selling everything, they've got ads on the back of Pods for TheoBars—you can't ClickDown a BulSheet that doesn't have a story on him. Never seen anything like it. He's Lindbergh."

"He's what?" asked Jules.

"Lindbergh—first solo flight across the Atlantic. You gotta Jump on Lindy one day. It's great. He flies this little plane out of St. Louis in America, all on his own. You can sit right there with him. He's so calm. He's a nobody. And then when he touches down in Paris, the world goes double pineapple. Everyone wants a piece of him. You've never heard of him?"

Both Jules and Gen shook their heads.

"Huh. And I thought we'd lost history in Billennium Fifteen. At least we've got the excuse that we were stuck on Mars for three millennia. You guys, you throw history away like it happened yesterday. Like it doesn't matter."

Jules was reminded of what Theo had told them about his Now, the world of Fifteen Billion and Seventy-three.

Everyone lived on Mars after being evacuated from Earth. And they'd only just started to come back to Earth to repopulate it. TimeJumping had been developed to help people rediscover the history of the planet that humans hadn't lived on for three thousand years. Instead it had turned into the biggest leisure activity for kids anyone had ever seen.

Franklin shook his head sadly. "Anyway, Theo is famous. He's the biggest StarLicker we've ever seen."

"StarLicker?"

"Yip, StarLicker. You know, famous, a celebrity. They rise so high, they can lick the stars. Wanna see some more?"

Jules started to say no, not that it hadn't been great to catch up with what Theo was doing, but it was getting late and maybe he really should be thinking about going home.

But Gen said, louder, "Yeah, what else have you got? How come he's lying about everything too? Does he ever mention us at all?"

Franklin had been scrolling through recordings as Gen spoke. "Nip, ooh, except for this."

Franklin ordered the Coat to show them more of Theo, and after the Coat turned itself into a snowsuit, showed them a clip of the Duke Ellington Orchestra, and measured Franklin's cholesterol and blood pressure, which actually rose while it was being taken, it finally did.

There was a close-up shot of Theo. He looked moody

and kind of handsome. His hair was sepia blue, and he was answering questions in an extremely serious way. The close-up widened and revealed that he was sitting up in the front of a lecture hall full of students. They were slouched down in their chairs as students do, and they were doing their best to look as though they didn't care, but they were all listening with rapt attention.

"So, you know," Theo was saying, "it's great to be here at the TimeMaster Academy for Advanced SiteSearching, and, I mean, I can't tell you guys anything about Entry/Exit Sequence or RLA Techniques, but I can just say this." Theo looked around the hall, pausing like a professional and adopting a deep and sincere look on his face. "You've gotta believe in yourself."

Theo was now nodding as if he'd just imparted something very personal and very real to the students. The footage was beautifully edited, cutting between close-ups of his hands, his fingers running through his hair, and attentive, gorgeous-looking students, and moody close-ups of Theo's face.

Jules's heart sank. He'd always felt like something had happened between Gen and Theo. Now, seeing Gen watch this clip, he wondered how he could compete with someone so well produced.

"When you're out there, and local time is running down," Theo was saying, as some gentle yet inspirational music began in the background, "it's just you and the universe. If you don't believe in yourself, you know, you're not going to find a way back home."

"Oh please, Franklin, what's happened to him?" asked Gen, a pained expression on her face. "He was a big enough tosser when he got here, but at least by the time he left he was nearly normal. No, don't tell me. He's just about to tell them, 'Hey it is true, you can live your dreams.'"

". . . live your dreams," echoed Theo on the screen.

Gen made a retching, groaning sound.

Jules grinned happily.

"Zip!" said Franklin. "I want you to hear this."

A girl with fluoro-lime hair stood up to ask a question. "Even though you were, like, kidnapped and all that," she said, "did you form any kind of relationship with them? I mean, the TimeHackers? Could you talk to them and all that?"

Theo swallowed and looked down. The room had gone very still and silent.

"There was a girl. She looked after me. I don't know that I'll ever see her again. Mil 3's a pretty hostile world, but I felt like we connected."

"What was her name?" the green-haired girl asked.

"Genevieve. Genevieve Corrigan," Theo replied quietly.

Franklin stopped the recording. Gen stood very still,

and Jules suddenly felt an overwhelming interest in the camellias by the front door.

"So the worst thing that happened to him with the evil TimeHackers here in Mil 3 was he got a crush on you!" Franklin poked a grimy finger at Gen. Then he shook his head ruefully. "There's something very wrong with this. It stinks like rotting valar juice, which doesn't stink that good when it's fresh. You can't just Jump somewhere visible by mistake. None of this was an accident. Maybe it wasn't meant to be Theo, but someone was thinking of coming here."

He slapped his hands together. "Rip! That settles it. I've had a brilliant idea. You're coming back with me!"

"Wh-what?" said Jules, looking up from the camellias.

"Lip, let's go! Let's Jump," said Franklin, grabbing them. "You can really help me. Quincy is planning something. I don't know what. But Quincy does not do anything for fun. He was never fun, he doesn't know how to have fun. If Quincy had your coordinates programmed into the JumpMan Theo used to get here, then all of this has something to do with you. So come on, let's go! Back in my Now, Quincy and Theo are about to make some huge announcement. The entire population's gone triple pineapple. You can take a peek and see what they're up to." He did the lizard thing with his eyes again. "So you want to help, or you just want to smooch on here for a while?"

Jules would have been pretty happy to smooch on, really. In fact, he'd been hoping to get that started when Franklin turned up. But the thought of going back to Theo's Time again was exciting. He didn't really know what Franklin was talking about, but how could he say no to another chance to TimeJump?